JERKS

Sara Lippmann

Mason Jar Press | Baltimore MD

Cover design and layout by Ian Anderson.
The cover photo, "Grant Moore and Alex Groetaers shake hands on tennis courts at Waskesin, Prince Albert National Park, Saskatchewan" was taken by Gar Lunney in 1952. Gar Lunney. Library and Archives Canada, e010949074

This book is set in FF Meta Serif.

Publishded by
Mason Jar Press
Baltimore, MD

Printed by Spencer Printing in Honesdale, PA.

Learn more about Mason Jar Press at masonjarpress.com.

STORIES

JERKS

WOLF OR DEER

When it rained, we played Would You Rather on the cabin floor. It was a game of tough choices. Would you rather eat sand or ash? Have snakes in your bed or spiders in your ear? We sat in a circle, knees touching, passed around potato chips that fit in our lips like duckbills. Would you rather drink your own pee or cow pee?

"Cow pee is a luxury beverage in certain parts of the world," Cynthia said. She got her period at nine and lorded her womanly knowledge over the rest of us in Bunk 12. I was not yet a woman.

"Not in my parts," said Marjorie. She blew her bangs. "Here's one. Would you rather go cannibal or starve to death?"

"No brainer," Sasha said. "I'd totally eat you."

A couple of squeals, a smashing of pillows, and the game took a turn. Eat or be eaten? Would you rather it in the ass or mouth?

"How about a pearl necklace," Cynthia moaned. She pressed her breasts together so the tops spilled out from her V-neck, large enough to be their own person. I stared.

"Stop staring," she said.

She wove toilet paper between her toes, shook a polish.

We were 14: bad skin and braces and too much hair. Hand job lessons with the shaft of a curling iron. We licked juice powder raw, stained tongues a cherry red.

I stood up. The floor creaked.

"Going somewhere?" Marcy Stein said. Everyone laughed. MC Hammer played from the boom box.

Rain pelted the roof. Activities were canceled. No swim, no archery. I stepped into my clogs without socks, mumbled something about my little sister.

"Homesick," I said. The screen whipped shut behind me.

Outside, camp smelled of sewage as if the septic tank had burst, mud splattering, heels sinking into the earth.

Fuck my little sister. My little sister was made for this place. My little sister was having the summer of her life.

Instead I ran to the gardener's cabin. He was not Israeli but had an Israeli name, which meant wolf or deer. He had an Israeli mother, which gave him built-in exoticism and the fraught, potentially tragic arc of army service. He was 23 or 25, scruffy, too old, but still in college because he'd had Hodgkin's lymphoma, had been this close to death. Now he was better, although his eyes were ashen, his skin a mustard yellow. I wondered if his disease would return; if it was still there, hiding somewhere dormant inside him. He lived alone in a row of huts called The Hutch.

That June I'd told my parents, You can't make me. Camp was a sports camp and I hated sports. Watch us, they said. When I got back I'd have two homes, not one. My parents said it like *Tada!* I was witnessing cell division, the miracle of mitosis.

What did I know from planting and watering and watching shit grow? At home we had a fish, but you can't split a fish. At camp, I took gardening. Side by side we worked, hands in the earth, long and rectangular as a funeral plot. He had skinny arms covered in fuzz that trapped the sun. He wore jean shorts, fringe on his thighs when everyone else wore these shiny wind sails called Umbros. His T-shirts said Megadeth. I chose mine carefully.

When he poured soil he'd look at me with those eyes, bold and unblinking as a deer. Outside the fenced bed, other girls knotted bracelets from safety pins hooked to their socks, unwilling to get dirty. Jessie, he said. I get you. My parents were breaking up because they no longer understood each other. Sometimes he'd pick me up and carry me across his shoulders down the hill like a canoe, like he might toss me in the lake and paddle me off in the sunset. My calves tingled, creamed and shaven.

"I could fit you in my pocket," he said. At night, I prayed to stay small.

Bunk 12 threw my swim towels off the line so they climbed with daddy long legs and stank of mildew. They dusted my sheets in baby powder and accused me of lice. I had Raggedy Ann sheets, which OK, fine, maybe was asking for it.

Whenever you need to escape, he said, come find me. I'd skip softball and nap in his bed, which smelled of grass and loam. If I left before he came, I'd leave a note, bubble letters. If he was home, I gave back rubs. He played music. There were checkers. We ate the yield from his garden: green beans, plum tomatoes. He called it our stash. In the mess hall he'd wink or do that snap and point with his hand, like a gun going off. Once, he offered me a beer from the back of his toilet. Initials carved into the rafters told stories of past lovers, other summers. When he hugged me and sniffed the top of my head, my whole body quivered like one of those novelty toys from the mall, a swirl of glitter.

That afternoon, I wore Marcy Stein's lace thong. It rode up my butt crack as I walked. I wore my black bra, bought from allowance.

I sucked a thin spray of Binaca, my feet sopping, but who cared. I was minty fresh.

When he did not answer, I went in. Inside it was dark, but I could see everything.

He sat up in bed, covers braced over chest.

"Jessie, this is Raquel from Waterfront."

I said I'd forgotten my stash.

"Take whatever's left," he said. "Hey, it's pretty wet out there. Use my umbrella or if you want, Raquel will run you back to your bunk."

But I just stood there dripping, leaving shit puddles on his floor, as he dangled carrots saying, "Which is it?"

HAR-TRU

The tennis moms are talking about *Polyamory*. It's a show. I've not seen it, but apparently it's a mash-up of *Housewives* and *Sister Wives* only the reality stars call their families pods and they are always naked and fucking, often in the shower, right on cable TV.

"I don't understand the shower," Linda says. "It's awkward, slippery. Once, I nearly twisted my ankle. I'm never lubed enough, my ass sticks to the curtain, Jack and I fight for the spigot, and we're only two people."

"What's to understand?" Felicity says. Now that she's divorced, she's enlightened; that is, she's getting it everywhere.

It is Sunday. Our kids take lessons on Sundays. Some people go to church but we sit in a bubble and watch our children chase a fuzzy neon ball. We watch for two hours. We've been watching for five years. I watch Simon for my soul.

Simon is their teacher. He is dark and hairy, movie star build, hot in a way that makes me feel things that are inappropriate. I could be his mother; I could be a lot of mothers; if I were his mother, I'd tell him to shave his neck.

"He looks like the actor from *American Psycho*," I said back when my daughter first started.

"Omigod, he does!" The moms agreed. "Those maniacal eyes. Don't creep us out, Amy, that's our children he's teaching."

They are not particularly great, our children—nothing you'd call gifted—but tennis keeps them busy and it is important to keep kids busy. Run them around and they'll run less at home. Simon, however, possesses a rare talent. Everyone adores him. Not just the natural athletes, the whole class: chubby boys, surly girls, the sore losers who throw rackets. Simon salts his coaching with life lessons. It's not all ready position, pivot, and swing.

"Believe in yourself," he'll say, dusting off their grips. "You can do it."

Other times, he'll say, "Dig deep. Show me what you're truly made of."

Today, at the outset of class, Simon comes up beside me pushing his ball cart. The wheels squeak.

"Hey, Amy. How's it going?"

The tennis center is like being inside a moon bounce. Sound gets bent and distorted. When Simon talks it's as if he's trying to reach me from within a distant tunnel, a paper towel tube through which, in another life, I'd blow smoke in dorm rooms to avoid RA detection. The bubble is fashioned with aluminum light fixtures that sway with the wind that seeps in through cracks in the seal. There is a constant buzzing, the hum of an insect trap. The light washes me out, casting me unfavorably. I blink and I blink.

He says, "Everything all right with you?"

Of course, small talk is normal. After years of watching, some things are inevitable. You strike up a connection. I mean, look at the moms and me.

"I can't believe you don't watch," Rebecca says. The moms pass around chips, gluten free. I shove my hand in the bag. "You have to watch. You're seriously missing out. What else are you doing in the bedroom?"

During warm-up, the kids hit short balls, long balls; they point and shuffle and pummel the overhead smash. They do this from the half court and baseline. They charge the net, volley. They vie for King of the Court.

"This one guy fucked his wife's new girlfriend against the cherry tree in their backyard, broad daylight, right in the nest of suburbia, cut bark and pink petals, for hours, in some kind of orgasmic initiation ceremony."

"Wasn't that episode ah-mazing?!"

"They weren't even skinny."

"Tattooed thighs rippling from that baby doll number."

"I'm all for body positivity but really."

"Monogamy," Felicity says, licking the salt off her fingers. "All but obsolete."

"It's a show," I say. "People act a certain way if they know others are watching."

"He's a suburban family dad! How many dads you know could ever act like that?"

The pod people all have day jobs, the moms report. Some of them are what you'd expect, acupuncturist, yoga instructor, sex therapist (duh), writer (double duh), but there are respectable jobs too; they are doctors and lawyers and kindergarten teachers when they're not busy practicing polyamory. They blend. They are all around us.

As moms, we watch from the sidelines. We bring water and snacks, hearty yet healthy, unlike the junk in the machine. We pity the new moms who don't know better. There are rules to the bubble. You can't just walk on at any time, but have to wait for the changeover. When you do walk, you can't stroll across the court like you own the place but defer to the players.

Occasionally I've seen people I've known, bowlegged men with bulging calves and bald heads shiny with sweat. They look different now than they once did, lung prints blotting their polos like Rorschachs, but who doesn't? Sometimes there's a flicker of recognition. "40-love," they'll spit, or "Deuce!" like it means something. The center's revolving door is resistant, strong as suction, a gasping for breath. You really have to push at it to move through.

My daughter, well, I can't say I blame her. She chants, "Simon is awesome! Simon rocks!" which may be my paraphrasing. My daughter claims no one says "awesome" and "rocks" anymore. She's 11, closer in age to him than I am, but she hangs on his neck like he's the uneven bars. Simon's a good sport. He'll swing her around. Toss, catch. Three years ago, it was sweet, maybe. But I tell her don't be desperate. She now insists on wearing a sports bra.

"What for? There's nothing there."

"I hate you," she says.

The first time your child tells you hurts the worst.

Which is to say: my problem is not with *poly*—I've been married 20 years— but with *amory*. Fucking is one thing. At night, my husband wants the light on but I insist on the dark. Some things, some people, are better left to the imagination. I have enough trouble loving as it is.

On the court, Simon instructs the kids to line up single file for a drill in quickness and reflex. He chucks balls at their heads.

"Duck!" he says. "You're going down!"

"Simon!" my daughter squeals. "You so totally nailed me!"

Every other minute, the moms say, the pod people are with someone new, sometimes three, five times a day.

"It's not only hot tub blowjobs and feather-weight whips, but conversation, coffee, cunnilingus. Group palm readings. Can you believe? They are actually committed to each other's feelings."

"Sounds exhausting," I say. The last I want is more demands on me, more hands tearing at my flesh like a store-bought chicken, more hungry mouths, more tender hearts to attend, much less flowers and chocolates and poetry and orifices and dicks.

"Don't knock it till you watch," Rebecca says. "Since Tom and I got hooked on the show, it's opened a whole new dimension onto our relationship. Now he wants to bring others in."

Felicity raises her brows. "Surprise, surprise."

When the kids scrape their ball hoppers along the surface Har-Tru, Simon joins me on the bench. I can smell his smell: clay meets armpit meets highlighter pen. The moms keep at it—but at a whisper. They prop purses on their laps like chastity belts. He lowers his chin toward me. I don't look away.

"So," I say. "How are you?"

"Great. Fantastic. Oh, Amy. I'm so glad you asked." Words rush like air from a new can of balls. "I'm having all these thoughts and moments and experiences and I–I–I should just cut to it, right?"

This is not unusual. In the past when I've asked Simon has told me, "To be honest, I could really use a friend right now." When my daughter first started taking lessons, he'd say my name over and over like a prayer until it took on meaning. Flopped his swampy curls on my shoulder, his ears pierced in little hoops, like a sporty George Michael. "How come no one tells you life isn't all it's cracked up to be?"

I didn't have the heart to tell him when someone asks *how are you* the answer is always: fine.

Instead I said, "Hang in there. Oh, my, would you look at the time. We must skedaddle to a birthday party."

By we I meant my daughter, as if I ever have a party to skedaddle to.

Once, he sat down beside me and started to cry. His shorts were tight and his nutsack was kind of poking out but when his nostrils quivered I gave him a tissue from a travel pack. Again he said my name.

"What is it with you," the moms said, "People just meet you and whoosh, raise the floodgates: life story pouring in."

Not people, I think. *Simon.*

During the break, the tennis moms stare. I can feel Simon in my face. How he sees me. How long it's been since anyone has seen me, since I've allowed anyone to see me like this. Heat floods my cheeks. He has a beard now, scruff, not hipster. He has hairy legs and tennis whites. He is talking about truth, living one's truth, honoring truth, staying true to truth.

He's 25 so it's almost endearing.

"I don't know if I should tell you this." His knee brushes my thigh.

"Tell me," I say.

"Microdosing," he whispers eagerly. There is an acai seed in his tooth from his energy smoothie. "LSD. I know it sounds dated, but you have that stoner vibe, like you've been through it all already."

"What's old is new," I say.

"I knew you'd understand! Oh, Amy, I've seen the light. I've unlocked the magic key to my heart and if I don't follow the giant luminous orb pulsing inside of me, then who am I, right?"

I try not to look at his crotch.

"What are we doing next?" my daughter asks once the balls have been picked up. She sucks on her water bottle, swings her ponytail, tilts boyish hips.

"Let's play." He taps her backside with his racket. "Round Robin? Free Bird? Tug of War?"

"Simon says!"

"You got it." He winks. To me he says, "Good talk."

In the poly world it's all about play parties.

"That's code for orgy," the moms say. "Threesomes, foursomes, ten in the bed. Supposedly, two men at once is like being boned by one supersized cock, can you imagine anything more American?"

"Or French," Felicity says.

I once spent the day with two tampons by mistake.

Linda crosses her legs. "Not after my labia surgery."

"But it's not just a free fuck for all," Rebecca says. "There are boundaries. Safe words and permission slips and things like *com-per-sion*."

"Does that involve cats?"

"When's the last time you felt a shred of pleasure, much less pure, unadulterated joy, from watching other people get off on each other? Kids today. Isn't that kind of sweet?"

Class is ending. Simon says, "Gather round, warriors. I have an announcement to make. I'm taking off for the summer. Europe, the Far East, who knows. It's about the journey not the destination. I'm not going to lie because even though you are young, you are people, and the truth is, love, warriors. Live free without limits or shame. For all the bunk on this planet you can't hide the truth. My truth is love and loving and—"

He whips his phone out of his pocket.

"Thanks to the Global Lovers app, I can swipe across continents for as many lovers as these hands can love."

At the word lover, the moms snicker. "Who even says that?"

I am blood red.

My daughter cries, "I hate Simon."

I open my arms to her. While I rub her hot back in small circles she says, "How could he do this to me?"

Her tennis pals sniffle and surround. "To us."

"Don't forget tonight's moms' night," the moms say as we pack up, gather coats and sheath rackets. It's a monthly event, sanctioned by dads. We're at the age where we have to schedule our fun, even if it makes us feel worse about ourselves. Moms' night is on the calendar. My husband will wait up in the bedroom while we crowd around high tops in our college jeans, drinking rosé, exposing back fat to unsuspecting patrons. The moms will lean in, "Now can we talk about Simon?" and I will angle myself accordingly and flap my mouth until it's empty.

Later, my husband will call me baby and reach, and I'll float up to the ceiling as he fills me, our bodies agile and alive and unwatched in the dark.

"Wouldn't miss it," I say. "Not for the world."

JERKS

We make beef jerky to distribute as gifts for the holiday season. Brian believes it is better to give a part of ourselves than it is to give cash, but I wonder if the recipients agree, if they see the gesture as heartfelt or narcissistic or stingy. We live in Brooklyn so we are hardly alone in this effort. Every year it is something: tins of granola, jars of dill pickles, artisanal yogurt by the biodegradable tub. Once, we tried bees on the roof but struggled with the yield.

Brian is on a real self-reliance kick.

"You can't count on anyone," he says.

Yet we are a team. Brian downloads the recipe from *A Gentleman's Guide to Survival*. While he trims the fat, the kids concoct flavor combinations: teriyaki, Cajun, sweet and sour. We also have original, not like we've done this before. After the beef marinates, we tuck strips into dehydrators that hum like a white noise machine. We wait and wait. Now we have all this shrunken meat. It is the color of dried blood, a scab that has been picked over and hardened. As I peel layers from the trays I notice: up close the jerky still looks raw. I suggest loading it back in the dryers.

Brian says, "It's not how it looks but how it feels." The meat feels tough. Still, I worry we'll give the mailman salmonella. Brian says, "That line of worrying will get you nowhere."

Packaging is my job. At the paper goods store I collect cellophane sleeves, ribbon to rip into curlicues, sticker labels, and a sparkle pen.

"How about The Jerks?" I propose as a name for our family enterprise. Brian tears a piece of meat with his teeth. He says, Ha-ha, in the way that makes it clear I'm not funny.

"The Herky-Jerky Man?" I try again but that is no better. I am a rusty brand manager; the older I get the more out of touch I become. Brian says there is almost a prideful stubbornness, a purposeful disdain to my unknowing, that I have no interest in giving people what they want. I'm not sure that's true or if I'm just out of practice. What does anyone want?

"A Heart of Beef?"

"Season's Meatings?"

"Main Game?"

"Jerk is the Word?"

"Now you're trying too hard," he says, so I leave off brainstorming, get back to the stuff and seal. I am my own assembly line. People are many things. In my life I have tried at turns to be thoughtful and kind but cannot offer a cost-benefit analysis of either.

As for erstwhile ambition—lately, doing the dishes is an accomplishment. When it gets dark at four o'clock, I pass out on the couch, fold over like a drunk, mid-snack, as if I'm not just bored but narcoleptic. There is no fighting it. This is heaven on Earth: being dead to the world. The TV blares. Between shows, the kids climb onto me like a pack of puppies, licking my face and tickling my armpits and when I don't respond, they poke. My skin is flushed and warm but doesn't spring back where their fingers push. The depressions remain. In meat terms that's an indicator of being past prime; I am no longer good.

Later at night, I can't sleep. Brian keeps the light on.

"Do you mind?" I say but he is reading about the anthropocene and sustainability. There is terror everywhere. He is researching safe spaces. Lying in bed with his combed hair and his tucked undershirt he looks like a cutout from the old Sears catalog. Bomb shelters once sold like erector sets, but I have no desire to survive that kind of disaster.

I climb into my daughter's bed. She is restless. I lie still. Her hand slaps my face; her watch ticks in my ear like a scolding. Time's a-wasting. It is a Swatch like I had as a child, when you swapped bands with boys to profess affection and loyalty. I assumed the brand went out of business. On the other side of the room, my son has something wrong with his heart. It goes "glub zlub" instead of "glub glub" which is probably nothing—"Innocent," the doctor says, "functional"—but I can't stop thinking *what if*. I strive for global perspective but there is my son going *glub zlub* and here is my daughter, kicking and kicking. I twine my legs around hers as if we might graft together, but she fights and flails then shoves me onto the floor.

For five nights in a row I sleep in their room. Brian is busy devising a plan to carry us off-grid. The question not *if* but *when*. The world is ending, that's a certainty, but if I were to say it, it'd be hysteria. Paranoia on me is practicality on him.

As a child, my parents unleashed their wrath on each other without concern for their neighbors, their children. I admire their anger. Mine is a different rage. It roils but has no place to vent. There are options, sure. Choices. I crawl into my son's bed, but it is toddler sized. My knees bang my chin. I feel like Alice in Wonderland pushing against her roof. My daughter continues to thrash. Tonight she sits up and wails, "I'm NOT going!" but it's just a dream; she plops back onto the heap of animals she is incubating and will not remember her protest in the morning.

Brian says autonomy is the greatest gift we can provide our children, and I agree, I don't wish dependence on anyone. People say I'm lucky. I look good in patriarchy. My daughter smells like sauerkraut and feet; she is not mango and whipped cream but ginkgo nuts, the chalky vomitus reek upon which I once twisted my ankle. That is her sweat.

When I'm not worrying about weak hearts, I worry about the elements. At six, my daughter has breast buds from who knows what's out there. Chemicals, environmental hazards, GMO, rBST, soy. You are what you eat, Brian says, which makes me a noodle in the dark recounting steps on a board game, sliding my pawn along the waxy plane to approximate the jagged moves of my youth: a zigzag, a seesaw, a ladder going up then down down down. My eyes are dry as a doll's. I lie there, but it's futile. The past haunts. The future creeps. My daughter catches me on the toilet. We talk about spilled blood and lost eggs, how losing is a regular part of life, something women celebrate around the world.

She looks between my legs. "How much have you lost?"

And I say: Think of it more like spring-cleaning, a shedding of what's not of direct use. While she sleeps, she slips a hand into the elastic of her pajama bottoms. Earlier, she'd found the word puberty in a book. "Will I catch it?" She wanted to know.

At breakfast, Christmas music plays on repeat. It plays on every station. Brian comes through the kitchen, humming "Do You Hear What I Hear?" It's amazing how cheerful he can be while preparing for Doomsday. I package the jerky for teachers, sanitation workers, UPS deliverers. Wrapped up they look like lumpy chocolate lollipops, as if I'd done heroic molds of One World Trade. Either way they are a disappointment.

My parents arrive for a visit. After all, it is the holidays. They bring eggnog and mellowed dispositions, provided they don't occupy the same room. My father is showering when I walk in to pee. Through the curtain I can make out his aging body: doleful breasts and shoulders heavy with hair, matted and slick as a seal. I slip out without flushing before he shuts the tap. My mother waits at the bathroom door, eyes bulging from thyroid, arms brimming with coated, battery-operated plastic.

"For the kids," she tells me.

I hide it all in a closet then throw on a dress. My parents are babysitting so we can attend a dinner party at our neighbors'. I don't know why we have to go when they never bother to curb their dog, but Brian welcomes the invitation to see how other people live.

When we get there, it is already loud and important. We bring our wrapped meat as party favors; place one on each plate. Everyone slides along wooden benches, farm style, even though we are in a basement apartment.

Brian places his hand on my lower back where a badass tattoo would go, if I had one. He does this without looking my way. It means,

Sit up straight. Immediately, he is roped into conversation. It is easy when you are Brian. People want to talk. I watch him throw back his head and laugh, eyes twinkling, chin jutting like Fred Flintstone. Sure enough, the blonde woman across from him leans forward to tell him about the sex book that changed her life. Actually, a trilogy. *Imagine!* Now she sells toys—for the boudoir. She wears a fur vest and permanent eyeliner and has a confession: she lives in New Jersey. But, she says, "Brooklyn women need me the most." A long crystal prong dangles from her neck, only it's more functional than mere charm, *wink wink*. Brian smiles and nods and says nothing about the dead animal draped across this woman's chest. Heat spreads where his hand is. I slouch deeper. I used to be afraid I'd turn out curved like Judy Blume's *Deenie* and no one would want to feel me up. Now, I realize that fear was misplaced. I'd marry. I'd become an adult.

The person to my right is discussing nineteenth century Islamic thought. He is an expert, and the person across from him is also an expert. I scan the table for familiar faces, the stay-at-home dad from the playground, the real estate broker with messy mascara, the bespectacled pair of enterprising Millennials who just moved onto our block, but we are on opposite ends. I examine my plate, cage-free protein aligned with designated pockets of seasonal greens and grains. It is stylish and unappetizing. If I cut and chew I figure I am absolved from conversation. I don't need to answer, *And what is it you do?*

With my mouth full, I observe the sex girl. She looks like my college roommate who also has a home business selling vibrators like Tupperware. On Facebook I liked it when she asked me to like it, but it's hard to believe she can be the same person who sat in bed fat and stoned all of freshman year. I never once saw her masturbate but Brian says, People change. You can do anything; become anyone you want if you put your mind to it.

It's late when the host and hostess rise to make a toast. They are in their 60s and have lived in Brooklyn the longest. Brian says we should entertain more, but what he really means is we should toast. Despite the news, there is much to celebrate on a local scale: a new traffic light, community mural, lending a helping hand. I peer through the red belly of my glass. The sex girl adds, Let's pray for world peace. We clink and clink and drink.

Back home, I take off my dress but Brian does not look up. He is already fired up about our next project. Canning! Salsa, jams and jellies. String beans. I'm not sure how that will help us survive, but Brian believes we've got to stay busy. Idleness is the kiss of death

"Shouldn't we wait for summer?" I say, climbing into bed. He faces the wall but it's not personal. We're not even arguing. I slide my fingers down his spine to where he likes it.

"No time like the present. You can start by making room for storage."

In the morning, I take care of the leftovers. Meat scraps for the neighbor's dog, sprinkles for the birds, shredded bits to fold into eggs. I swear the jerky stash seems to be growing rather than diminishing. In certain light, the dried ends gleam green. I can't look at it anymore. I don't care what's a waste. When my parents leave, I dump junk drawers and shelves, organize chests and closets, clean out the pantry, make stacks and piles and heaps. My kids trail behind me, the ragged edges of their security blankets sweeping a trail of dust bunnies. "Is it recycling day?" and "That's Daddy's," but there is a rapt fury to my focus. I drag out trash bags, jumbo-sized for lawn debris, and shake them open. My kids stretch the mouths wide as a pit. I climb in. I'm not interested in donation. I throw out what we don't need.

IF YOU'RE LUCKY, THIS COULD BE YOU

Brittany tells Shania to come to yoga. You better fucking be there, are her words. Since she got clean and Zen, she is on her sisterly high horse. It is hell.

"Don't be late, bitch," she says, handing Shania an apple. "For your own damn good."

The school bus takes forever, but Shania's dad's either sleeping or out with the truck, so she shoves her slipper socks into boots and walks the half mile down River to Main. The sun is bright and the day is cold, but Shania's used to the sting. Her breath looks like smoke, nothing clever, but she holds it for as long as she can, her exhale always shallower than her inhale. The clock at the credit union (*America First!*) reads three degrees Fahrenheit, minus sixteen Celsius, which is like, who can mend the planet when no one can even agree on how to measure air? The bookshop has closed, as has the crystal beading café, but the Great Wall of China is always empty and open. Rings ice her hands, ankhs and turquoise moons, studs punched from lobe to cartilage. She piles on all the jewelry she owns at once, even though it discolors her skin. Her fingers are pink as runts by the time the bus slows and flips its arm, not that there's any traffic. School is on School Street, down the road from the Mountain Wellness Spa, whose kale-eating, soul-seeking clients keep the whole town afloat.

Her mom did housekeeping until Brittany took over, until she got busted, but Mountain Wellness believes in second chances. Thanks to their outreach initiative, Brittany has been to rehab, been through yoga and mindfulness training, and moved to kitchen staff, where she spends her mornings dicing carrots and deboning poached chicken for slaw. Certification hours complete, she's now teaching her first class, a gentle vinyasa on Thursdays, open to the public and not just guests in their fat-sucking spandex and fur boots. All week, Brittany has been slamming her gong in preparation. At 22, her life is on the up and up.

School's fine, whatever. Shania is in ninth grade and likes art, likes building stuff from a picture in her head. When she designed a napkin holder in sheet metal, her father called her a girl after his heart; said, Maybe next time you can make something more practical, but they're no longer allowed to do ashtrays. She likes drawing, too; she draws on her jeans and shoes, doodles concentric shapes that inevitably look phallic or vaginal, sparrows and squirrels and brook trout, shingles of scales. Sometimes she wishes she had more imagination, a fantastical, outer space dreamscape in which to lose herself, but Shania never strays much from reality. Brit's boyfriend, Duck Creeley, once told her she was real good, like tattoo-level, but he was high at the time, and Brit said the moron wouldn't know truth if it ran through his veins, and Go wash your face, ink's blotting your chin.

It's Black History Month, so Ms. Tibbs has decorations on the wall of Frederick Douglass, Harriet Tubman, Rosa Parks, the illustrations scalloped like postage stamps, eyes fixed on the middle distance. Shania can count on fingers the number of Black people who've come through Northern Vermont, but she doesn't get how anyone would embalm themselves in such calm, least of all those fighting injustice, which may be the point: they didn't choose their images. Rage till you're blue and still your story gets usurped and rewritten. Ms. Tibbs dims the lights, presses play. It's the same each year. When Martin Luther King Jr.'s voice rings out *I have a dream*, half the class lowers their heads down on desks.

Out the window it's started snowing, and the plow's coming through, emergency lights flashing and beeping as it scrapes and reverses, reverses and scrapes, dropping a trail of rock salt. Tonight, she and Brit will share the bed by the space heater, which blows loud as a hand vac, splitting her lips, but it's the only spot of warmth against the wind. We will never be satisfied, King says, and Ms. Tibbs pauses the tape to say, Repetition is an effective rhetorical strategy. In her own life, Shania has seen the same things said and done over and over and it doesn't seem to persuade anyone to be better. It snows all goddamn day. From afar, the flakes look fluffy and white, but up close her perspective changes. Up close, the snow is heavy and gray.

Her mother died from snow. One thing leads to another. Skiing six years ago, not that she had any business skiing, but she'd been in one of her states at the time, getting loaded and knocking off work and leaving them at dinner to fend for themselves. Her mom loved that phrase, like her family was a pack of scavengers. Be creative, she'd say. You'll come up with something. Shania was in third grade and came up with omelets and canned hash for dinner. Brit was a junior and came up with booze. Her family was a seesaw. Her dad sank when her mom went flying. Cash Mitchell was a family friend. Cash took her to the handcrafted brew pubs and farm-to-table tourist traps, rode her around in his Sno-Cat grooming bumps to smooth corduroy, her mom coming home as Shania was waking, cheeks flushed and alive. Aren't you bored out there, Shania asked and her mom said, We play music, there's heat in the cab, always the chance of a mountain lion. Can you imagine how lonely Cash would be without company? Later in the season, once the base melted and select trails were lit for night skiing, Cash was transferred to lift operation. Come on, Marie, he said, what good is life if you don't risk it. First run and her mom caught the tip of her ski on a root sticking out from shoddy cover and snapped her femur clean. The injury, however, is not what killed her. What killed her was every subsequent effort to nullify the pain.

Occasionally in winter, their dad barrels in from wherever he's been, pops a stew can on the stove like a cranberry mold, and says, Let's build the world's biggest fire. If Shania doesn't set out for kindling, he'll wield his axe through the back woods, which makes her nervous. Too many people around her wielded dangerous things, hacking at the world like it was too small and not big enough for them.

On these nights, Shania spreads car blankets on the living room floor, and tells her dad they don't need to light up anything. Come, she says, gently, as if he were a dog that's strayed. Come inside, Daddy. She waits. Shakes out Parcheesi, I'll beat your pants off. Eventually, he lumbers back in.

At lunch, the cafeteria ladies hand her a ham and cheese and she sits at a corner table picking at it. Matt, Lacey, and Carlene sprawl out beside her, which allows her to disappear in their chatter. Mouths move but it's background noise. A bunch of seniors have been slurping a tray of vodka Jell-O somebody brought in and have gone feral, scooping up the slippery cubes of red flesh with their claws, sucking it down and howling. Billy Latham snorts gelatin through a straw and the table laughs, it's so obvious, but lunch monitors do nothing about it. Billy gets away with everything. He's got this white-hot current running through him no one can resist. His brother is in prison and his sister is in prison and someday Billy will be in prison, too, but he lives out Shania's way and if he sees her waiting for the bus sometimes he'll give her a ride; other times he'll drive right past her.

Billy's in her math class because for all his electricity, he's not that bright. Ms. Meehan flirts with him like it's a big joke, Billy being in algebra for the fourth time. Leans at the edge of her desk in her camel cable-knit turtleneck, staring him down in their own private language, as if Billy's already of age, which for all Shania knows, he may be. Ms. Meehan isn't from Vermont, she's a student teacher completing her masters up at the college. Like the rest of them, she'll last through June, stock up on maple syrup then move on to Burlington or Boston, or strike gold with central New Jersey.

Today, Billy strolls into class chewing a gummy bear the color of champagne and Meehan says, Stop right there. She calls him Mister. Shania feels a twinge in her thighs watching them, Meehan's suede boots raising her to his chest height, chin to chin, like they're squeezing a balance ball between them. I was not born yesterday. He shoots her a knowing grin. It's just candy, he says. Cross my heart. He flashes his dimple and she sticks out her hip. It's like they're playing a part, trying to impress the other, performing for the whole class. We can do this the easy way or the hard way. Billy says, How would you like to do it? Very hard? And Meehan shuts her eyes to keep from blushing, palm out, which is when Billy tosses the baggie into the room and Shania catches his stash and houses it.

She sucks off their sugar coating first. Granularity gives way to glycerin, a sweet glaze. Then she swallows the bodies. They are watermelon, bubble bath, a box of White Claw; they are a summertime party.

The bell rings. In study skills they're practicing personal statements, *Describe yourself in ten years*, but Shania's already written hers, so she goes to the bathroom then out the double doors through the parking lot to the bus circle. Druggies wear Guatemalan fanny packs and smokers wear fingerless gloves, but there's plenty of overlap. Everyone dresses from the same two stores. Shania throws over her hood and stands at the curb picking shake from her pockets as the snow lands fatly, waiting for the bears to kick in, feeling nothing and nothing and nothing and then feeling all too much.

When Billy pulls up in his truck, she gets in. She needs to be at Mountain Wellness by 4:30, but what is time. He asks her if she's okay. She nods and her head rolls off her shoulders and under the seat, like that song her mom used to sing, on top of spaghetti all covered with cheese. A lost meatball, that's what she is. That was dope what you did, Billy says, but language is lodged in her throat, and when she reaches for words, they scatter and retreat, burrowing deeper until she's valleys below. Her palms buzz, she can't stop rubbing her thighs.

"Didn't know you were such a little badass," he says, *ass* slithering off his tongue, but here comes his hand clamping hers in his shell. Her fingers are hermit crab legs. She wiggles them. There are cat prints on her leggings. When he snaps them, they pounce, the closest to a pet she'll ever own, and it's hilarious.

Subway takes all of five minutes. Trevor is working, so he gives her a botched order, and she makes quick work of it; the meat is pink meat, and the bread expands inside her like a sponge. Trevor says, How's your sister, and Shania shrugs. She pulls a strand of hair from her mouth that's gotten caught on the food. Trevor scratches his jaw. Tells her to come by sometime. There's an open scab on his arm in need of attention. She nods at it but he doesn't catch on. Blood, she thinks. Your inside is leaking out. Kind of like, your epidermis is showing. Only she's not saying any of it. When she steps outside, Billy says, What about me? Shania throws up her hands. You really must be wasted, he grins, clearing a swirl of mayo from her lip. She guzzles her Mountain Dew. Frost coats the window. It looks like branches. Everything looks like something else. She presses her cheek to it. When she opens her eyes they are at Duck Creeley's barn.

"Wait here," Billy says but Shania is not waiting in an ice-cold truck. Billy's gonna die, she can feel it. She should warn him, but boys like Billy do what they want. (At her mother's funeral, Cash Mitchell said: We all die, kid.) She doesn't want to get too close to the barn. Even with the windows boarded, the smell of Duck's cooking hits her behind the teeth, plastic burning, so she opens the cab and walks off, her feet like poured Windex in the snow, gummies dissolving in slow release. She imagines them stretching and unfolding, opening inside her like Shrinky Dinks, like that Saturday morning cartoon. Instead of a bear with a cloud on her heart, she is a cloud with bears in her belly. Only after she's been on the road for a while does she realize she's swinging Billy's keys. Oh. Well. Decisions.

She adopts a stick, drags it through the snow, slush and gravel, looks up at the sky. Her PE teacher, Mr. Reynolds, introduced them to cloud appreciation. Brandished his International Cloud Society membership card to outright mockery. *Someday, you'll wish you belonged to something.* That fall, they lay on the track field, arms folded beneath their heads as the earth spun, trees bursting with color, clouds pretty as poodles, while Reynolds taught them cirrus, cumulus. At first, it felt ridiculous, just watching, but then no more ridiculous than anything else. Lenticular she'd known from the Disney hologram puzzle her dad brought home from Goodwill the year she turned eight.

But today is overcast. Today is too foggy to differentiate one cloud from the next.

Cars roll by. Shania counts then stops counting. She's tired of walking but there's no choice but to walk. The shoulder is a tightrope she teeters along, dipping one foot then the other, like any second the white line will curve out and she'll slip and the ground will fall away. The light is flat, but if she keeps on she'll hit the river and from there, the distance will even out. She tells herself the feeling will pass like all other feelings, which sparks another song: *Winston tastes good like a cigarette should*, a clapping game her mom taught her, all the hand motions, thumbs at the ears: *Ooohh aaah. Want a piece of pie*. Her mom wore a yellow halter-top in summer. Lipstick called Silver City Pink eroded to a sharp, iridescent nub. Her shoulder blades stuck out like wings. A hawk soars across the sky.

When she arrives at yoga, Brittany is setting the mood with candles and incense. Did you get fucking lost? Brit seethes, but Shania is winded, cheeks slapped. having run the last bit, she still can't answer. Well, at least you're here. Grab a bolster, a blanket, grab whatever you need. Leave your shoes. Class is about to begin.

The yoga mat looks like a long, blue tongue. Panting, Shania lies on it, waits for her body to still. The mat smells cunty, like a curled maxi pad left to wilt in a gym locker. Around her lie ladies from Mountain Wellness, a few men, gray hair and ponytails, bowed, hairy knees. Brit's supervisor wears genie pants that flap at the crotch like a pet door. The woman arranges herself on a buckwheat meditation cushion, tapping a notebook as if poised to keep score. Students warm up by grabbing their feet like babies, rocking from side to side. When they roll toward her, Shania feels them staring, feels them thinking *they really let in e-v-e-r-y-o-n-e*, but she is no mind reader. For all she knows they're not thinking of her at all. Everyone thinks mostly of themselves. She rolls up. Picks a hangnail. Strokes her hair.

It is long and thick and swings down her back like a horse. Brit envies it. Brittany is nothing special, which she offsets by calling attention to herself in other ways. Twenty tattoos she's still paying off, from sharks to lightning bolts the size of King Triton, an iridescent Man of War menacing her lower back. Brit's never even seen the ocean, but people covet what they can't have. Shania has a perfect Cupid's bow. Our little porn star, Brit said. At night, Shania cups her new breasts, and it's a comfort, to hold herself like this, soft and warm, full of possibility.

Life didn't stop after her mom's accident. Shania needed pencils, needed milk money, needed a ride. Brit never signed up for caretaker at 16, not like there was much caretaking going on beforehand. Life sucks the life from you, pushes you into certain lanes. Patterns repeat. Shania watched dolphins flip through the air on YouTube over and over without a click prompt or reward. Maybe all behavior could be taught. Her dad has never ventured south of Windsor. All the country he needed was right here. Her mom's scripts were a doctor's order. Death, a mere casualty of conditioning.

Welcome to Flow, Brit says from the dais. She's wearing a chocolate brown camisole with no bra, a tunnel of sweat running down her breastbone. Once Shania sees it, she can't stop seeing. Her gaze is a laser to her sister's cleavage. When Brit was in a bad way, she cleared out the cash from her dad's toolbox and stole Shania's unicorn sweatshirt, butchered the neck and sleeves. She got real skinny and her face pitted like a planet, but recovery has wrought such buoyant magic upon her that now, even in her tenuous state, Brit radiates a hope that's almost convincing.

The room is strung up in little white lights like the kind Mountain Wellness threads through its holiday privet. Brit leads them in breathing, three parts, nose and mouth, and it's rich, Shania has to bite her lip to keep from snickering. The collective exhale is so loud it sounds fake. Brit has them close one nostril then the other like they're playing the body recorder. All Shania can think of are vapor particles latching onto other particles. In elementary, her class played Jailbreak on the hardtop. Eventually, the children all broke apart.

At 15, Shania has seen plenty of death. Barn accidents, thresher accidents, car accidents, freak accidents. Lang Boone choked on a hotdog. ODs, too many to track. Stasis could be a killer. But then her mom died from impulsivity. Goes to show, her dad said, then never completed his thought. Shania doesn't mind death but protracted dying. If only her mom had gone on impact, boom, smack into a tree.

The floors are heated, so nice. Shania stretches her arms off the mat, sweeping them along the wood like snow angels, so shiny and smooth she'll never leave. She'll sleep here in the studio, bask in its buttery light, the smells of pine and orange soda. After class, Brit will take her to the back where there's an electric kettle and they'll break ramen and curl up on Mexican blankets, shower in the spa bathroom with its everlasting supply of lotions and soaps; she'd do it, too, if it weren't for her dad, move into Mountain Wellness like that pregnant teen in a big box bathroom, hide out and wait, and allow herself to become some rich lady's charity case.

In the past, she'd come home to gas leaching from the stove, the whole room reeking like eggs, someone having forgotten to shut the pilot. Close call, but a call nonetheless. Shania relied on the law of probability: like, she couldn't lose her mom and blow up her home in the same year, but apparently, she could lose her mom, her dad could lose his job, and they could all nearly lose her junked-up sister, though that was pushing it. Only so much a character can bear, but her life is not a goddamn movie. How's this for plot? Fires erupt when people aren't paying attention. The space heater, with its meager promise, melted everything in its path. Amber bottles into warped clocks, like the Salvador Dali poster in the art classroom, the photos she'd seen of Zion National Park. Someday, Shania will make it to Utah. Even Brit said, You need a trip, Daddy, when she stopped using. Where am I going, Muffin? He answered, then went to the bar, or sat at the trailhead, or parked on the tracks and listened for the slow daily rumble of a distant train.

"Set an intention," her sister instructs, "bring hands to heart center." It takes Shania a minute to figure out what's wrong with her speech. Why does her sister sound so funny? Like Yoda. Shania can't stop fixating on it until she realizes: Brit's lopped off the articles. Why isn't anyone correcting her? Hand to foot, elbow on knee, ribs stacked on knee, left hand on right thigh, like she's playing Twister in the den and it's her mom's birthday and someone spilled the punch and someone else, Uncle Mick, is reaching through Brit's legs, and everyone looks square at his hands then twists the other way.

But she's got to give it to her. When Brit says stand (rise in mountain, is what she says) the yogis stand, and Shania wishes she knew what it was like to have people listen to her. Brit is like Billy in that way, commanding the whole room with her swan folds, her up and down dogs. Her body moves with a driven grace, and Shania tries to keep up, but Brit is fast, Shania's socks are slipping, and the Subway sandwich is burbling around, so she punks out, flays on all fours like a splat ball from the Dollar General, a calf on unused legs.

The poses keep coming. Brit dives; they dive. When Brit shape shifts into a camel, a pigeon, a Goddess, a warrior, the Mountain Wellness people follow in kind, regarding Brit with an awe saved for celebrities, like she's never been jailed for possession.

Now Brit deserts her dais to circle the room, offering adjustments and modifications. Students relax into her hands, sighing heavily, her touch a salve for their ills. Her spine is so straight it's as if someone is yanking a string from her crown. She hisses into Shania's ear, "You're an embarrassment. Can't you at least try?"

In front of her, a man bridges out with a beard mossed like Cash Mitchell, Grateful Dead T-shirt, pelvis thrust like a saber toward the ceiling. Billy Latham was going to goddamn kill her for walking away with his keys. Punish her good and then what. Move onto somebody else.

"Pay attention," Brit says. "If you're lucky, this could be you."

Last summer, Shania had a job distributing towels at the Wellness pool. Guests wanted extra even as they claimed to give a shit about the environment, the lush green hills, the sunrise views. It's like living at the top of the world, they said, and she smiled, patted the hot, quilted terry. Or at the edge of it, they whispered, sandals thwacking. Can you imagine the desolation in winter?

Outside, it's already gone dark. When Brittany offers the option to hang out in child's pose, Shania takes it, her stomach resting on her thighs. How much more snow? How would he croak, Billy? She feels queasy, like the room is spinning or she is spinning around the room. She doesn't know which. Maybe she's just sobering up. Sometimes, she still dreams of her mother. Her smell, garlicky fingers; her scratchy, below-the-surface laugh. On cold nights, she'd put their socks in the oven so they'd wake up to something loving and warm.

In lotus position, Brittany sits with a purple velvet book in her lap, poetry, or some Bible of spells. Savasana may mean Corpse Pose, but I like to think of it as a letting go to make room for the new. Rid yourself of the dead, Brit says. Lie down. Lying Shania can do. Brit raises her gong. As the sound echoes through you, inhale all that beauty and knowledge; exhale the clarity you've gained.

A BEASTLY THING

Then Skylar says breastfeeding makes her horny. It is a mindless slip. They've been on the couch—she and Ralph's dad, Kevin, talking about monkey bars, carrot sticks, safe plastic; i.e., talking about nothing at all, baby Emma in her arms sucking away, the boys in the next room sucking thumbs on railroad-themed bunk beds. There is no reason for the confession, a provocation, for the sudden burst (she is nursing, she is always nursing), her words muscling from her lips as if on their own volition, like runaways thumbing it to freedom; once out, there is no turning back.

Kevin places his beer on the side table. Skylar holds herself still, as if stillness could camouflage, as if, like sighted prey, stasis might make her disappear. If only she had one of those curtains other mothers wear: hooter, heifer hiders—but she is too late; she is already seen. She can hear Kevin's breath quicken, his body inching closer to hers on the couch, the sautéed meat and onion cloud of him. Tacos, earlier. Skylar stares into the fire. The flames mellow to a slow burn while heat rises, bathing her body in a fresh hormonal sweat, her breasts on display like an offering, an obscene feast of veiny moons swelling up to her chin. It is inevitable. She sits there cross-legged, preposterous. Leggings cling to her postpartum body, the elastic cutting into her ankles, still thick, even though it's been months since she's given birth. How did it go? *What do babies, leggings, and drunks have in common? They don't lie.* She tries to smile. A dull ache courses through her, spine rooting into the couch while the rest of her is loosening, leaving her feeling both empty and full, tethered to her child, so that even if she wants to flee there is no choice but to remain as she is, arms occupied, body alert yet exposed, and therefore, culpable: a mother at her most mammalian.

Facts. Kevin is a good guy. Skylar was happy to go away with him. The entire weekend, hatched by their spouses, had been a done deal. She and Kevin should go. Do something. Melanie, Kevin's wife, would be working, Doug as well. Melanie was a trial lawyer and Doug had a new start-up to launch. They had to work. They always had to work. *Someone had to work*—to cover the costs of raising mouths in New York, to pay for things like this fully appointed log cabin VRBO. They spoke as if Skylar and Kevin were employees, charges under adult care, requiring permission. This was the fate of stay-at-home parents. When the breadwinners snapped fingers, they obeyed. It was a long weekend, devoted to a dead president. Why not head out of the city and breathe some country air, make vats of chili and teach the boys to ski? What else would they do? Sit around the cold slips of their apartments waiting and waiting—for what?

Before they left for Vermont, Kevin did the shopping. He stocked up on firewood, packed extra bedding. He bought snacks and gummy worms and portable games for the drive. The last thing he wanted was to increase Skylar's burden. He said this gallantly, in a tone that reminded Skylar of her own father, who went out of his way for her mother, bending himself backward without actually being helpful, until her death when Skylar was 13.

"Let me take care of you," Kevin said. "Think of it as a mini vacation, a spin at the spa. You deserve it."

Skylar didn't know what she deserved, but Kevin had a minivan. On the drive, the radio went in and out. Sometimes it was Buddy Holly and sometimes it was Little Feat. Skylar felt lulled by the car's easy movement. As soon as they hit the FDR, Emma fell asleep, unbothered by the boys' chatter. Skylar's lids grew heavy but Kevin twisted the radio dial, shook out a bag of chips. Night came early on the road, switch-backing through the mountains, but he wanted to talk in the dark. He wanted company. He was driving, after all. It was only fair. She'd never told him the story; how did she and Doug meet?

"In the neighborhood," Skylar said. Which was partly true. It certainly sounded better than, "he was a customer," although that is what he was. When she worked at the gourmet outpost in brownstone Brooklyn, Doug frequented her charcuterie. She sliced samples of prosciutto thin as stained glass. She handled logs of bresaola and homemade duck sausage and ham hocks and wedges of raw sheep's milk. She paired them with little pickles. Back then, Skylar was a dish. At 25, she didn't live in the leafy neighborhood of her employment, but in a hip enclave beneath the BQE, where it was commonplace to hang out in a stranger's loft with one man's hands on her legs, another up her shirt, where possession was bourgeois and bodies ran together in a collective state of reckless glamour, where life was buzzing and beautiful and endless and unknown, where she contemplated gastronomy tattoos on the bowls of her ribs until the novelty ran out.

Everything came down to timing. Doug kept coming back, so she kept serving him, holding up slices of meat on squares of wax paper. She had to rise onto her toes to feed him. Swaths of deli became teasing long tongues, then dental dams. They laughed across the counter. She never asked who he was entertaining with such luxury goods, if he just ate that way. Never did he take a ticket number, even when the counter was mobbed. Doug was not one to wait. He was a well-tucked man in a tapered suit and Italian brogues. She was pierced and aproned, a lattice inked up her wrist that did not lead to anywhere. He said, "How do you keep a body like yours in a place like this?" Soon, they were fucking against the wall of the freezer.

That's how they met. It was exhausting to think about now, much less recount.

Skylar said, "We had similar taste."

Taste, as she understands it, can be split into two camps: People either worship the mirror—that is, they want to fuck themselves—or their direct opposite. On the surface, Skylar and Doug could not be more different, but both relished the scent of strangers; found anonymity an undeniable thrill. In the shop they could be anyone. They did not discuss life goals. Sex was surprising and standard, erotic yet by the book, which is how Skylar liked it. For Doug, it was crazy. Skylar grabbed his tie and Doug said, "You're crazy," not because it was wild or inventive nor because of any questionable sanity on Skylar's part, but because, like her, Doug fantasized the unfamiliar, because contrast cast the self into relief.

"Shut up," she'd say, shoving her metal-balled tongue down his throat to get him to quit narrating the play-by-play. Behind the counter, in the storage closet. Then in the park: damp floor of the boathouse and again in the open, atop a bed of wilted magnolia. In the elevator to his prewar apartment, beneath a shower head that attacked from all sides like a car wash. Naked on his rooftop under the stars.

When Skylar got pregnant it was sexy, at first. She wore tight clothes to show off her shape, to show how successfully—how triumphantly—she'd been fucked. Then they were married and suddenly she was a wife and a mother, adulthood catching up on her. Luke was born. Again she got pregnant, which was about as adult as rollerblading without a helmet. Who even rollerbladed anymore? Her first trimester with Emma, Doug's breath smelled like horse in the rain, which made her wretch, she couldn't bear his insistence in her mouth, his tongue swiping left then right, those big slimy teeth clanging against her, so she averted his gaze lest she throw up. Then the tables turned. When she grew fat and alive he grew gun-shy, afraid he'd somehow poke the unborn eyes out of the kid. But then, all men overestimated themselves, and every mother had an opinion, which they foisted upon her, unasked, wherever she turned. Her panic rose. *What was she doing?* Ah, but this was normal. There were mothers everywhere, mothers proselytizing like subway preachers: Pipe down. Ease in. Accommodate, accommodate. To what? Expectations, self-sacrifice: the daily rhythms of life.

At 32, Skylar has one at her breast and another down the hall, her years before Doug reduced to distant memory, a onetime dream, a snippet she'd overheard third hand. Skylar looks into her arms. Emma's breath rises and falls wetly alongside hers. Skin to skin. Her chest heaves. No. Her *bosom.*

Usually, when Emma goes at her like this, Skylar can detach and float up. It is easy to disconnect. Her body is no longer hers. Whatever pride she once harbored toward her daughter—squishy thighs fed entirely by her milk supply!—has dissipated. She nurses out of laziness, not righteousness. Lifting her shirt requires less of her than getting up to fix a bottle. Doug's mother disapproved. No one did it in her day. Breastfeeding was reserved for peasants, she said. It was bad enough Doug had married a peasant. Once, Skylar peed with the door opened and Doug said he'd never seen a woman—much less a mother—on a toilet. So much for mystery! She was a human pacifier. Emma is already on solid food. Emma doesn't need her. What she needs are oatmeal and bananas, sweet potatoes. Jars are fine. Emma will take whatever she gets.

But there is no escaping herself with Kevin there, eyeing Skylar like some exotic new fruit. He relights their joint, smoothing its creases with his fingers. Kevin has not witnessed her body turned out like the head of a plunger. Kevin sees only the curve of her shoulder, the glint of collarbone in the lamplight. Skylar closes her eyes. Her muscles relax, and there it is, like a wave: desire recklessly crashing into her thighs.

No one had told her about this.

No one had told her about sitz baths and Epsom salts, compression underwear either. The whole species would be extinct, if secrets of parenthood were ever to seep out to the not-yet-procreating set. It was a coup simply to be alive. No one told her about the pain and hurt, which her own mother hid until it consumed her. No one ever said she'd be dry where she'd once been wet, tender elsewhere; horribly lonely yet never alone, there would be always someone attached and clawing. No one told her about erasure or conflation. That she could sate her daughter's hunger and her own at the same time.

Kevin holds the joint to her lips and she pulls on it, nodding when her lungs are full. She exhales. Emma has fallen asleep. The slightest shift and her baby slips off, her mouth fishing away at the air, unaware that it's missing Skylar's nipple, slick and pronounced as a giant hemangioma, a birthmark to be iced and excised for pathology.

Kevin stubs out the roach.

"Mother may I?" he says, zeroing in.

She no longer looked Doug in the face. Every time (a grand five times) he nuzzled up to her, she'd turned, offering her back instead, dimples for eyes, the arch and swell of her bottom the most generous part of her, the only part not yet claimed, he took his pleasure briskly, her body leaking afterward like a broken toy.

He has still not forgiven her for hacking off her hair. Baby Emma gripped everything. Earrings, chains. Streaky blonde locks. The cut made Skylar feel ten pounds lighter, marginally free.

"Feel," she said, taking his hand to the buzz at her neck.

He recoiled. "How could you do that to yourself?"

As if she needed permission, as if it were a personal affront, Doug retaliated with a whisky fetish and a chaotic back tattoo. Skylar pictured him bending over his office assistant, Katya. Katya was 23 and from Romania. Katya wore knee socks and pleated skirts. Katya said things like "In my country." If Doug weren't fucking her, Skylar would be almost disappointed. Who would pass up the opportunity?

With his big hands, Kevin scoops Emma into his arms, rendering Skylar irrelevant. She watches him tuck her daughter into the port-a-crib. If he were conventionally attractive, they would not be here together. Melanie would not have released him. But he wasn't and she had, and the weekend so far had been a holiday movie: fresh pine and maple, the cabin everything a getaway could be. In the morning, Kevin made pancakes and took the boys skiing and Skylar sat in the lodge watching families reserve tables with heaps of wet mittens. Even if Emma weren't crawling around the slushy floor, clapping spoons together, Skylar wouldn't be skiing: she did not grow up blowing this kind of money to freeze to death. It was fascinating, though, how these strangers bragged about their gear, electric boots and fog-free goggles; flapping open wilted maps and running their ketchup fingers along the trails. She burned her tongue on the foam of hot chocolate.

"Hush," he says, putting Emma down. "Baby, baby."

Kevin hops back on the couch, scooting along the length of cushions. Head cocked, eyes watery as a boy she once knew, who taught her to skateboard in a value store parking lot, Kevin is not an average dad but an old dad, he must be nearly 60, his nose pug-like, the shadows of youth faint in the contours of his jaw. If Skylar has dropped out of the workforce, Kevin is retired. His hair, white and thick, combed for the nightly news, yet there is a Christmas spirit about him. The buttons of his flannel strain. Skylar has forgotten to snap the folds of her nursing bra. Her breasts poke through the corn holes.

"Where were we?" he says.

He and Melanie were an unlikely couple, too, Kevin volunteered on the long drive up from the city. Not that Skylar had asked. She wasn't even listening. Her cheek against the frosted window, she welcomed the cold, murmured the minimal sounds of agreement. It was OK. Sometimes people needed to talk for themselves.

"To know her is to love her," Kevin said. Skylar doubted that. But then, she barely knew Melanie.

"Some men get intimidated by her success, but that's because they're insecure. Not me. I live to serve: to cook and clean. Errand is my middle name." He said it boastful, without a shred of irony.

"Consider me the world's greatest wife."

Indeed, Skylar said. She called Melanie a lucky lady.

They'd met the previous fall on Luke's curriculum night. (What kind of "curriculum" could there be for four-year-olds?) The room was stale and hot. Skylar couldn't squeeze her pregnancy into the mini chairs of primary colors and drink apple juice with the other parents, knees banging the desks, so she stood along the wall of the classroom beside Kevin, whose paunch presented a similar obstacle.

"We're twins." He held his belly. Skylar tugged at the stretch of her skirt. It was too short in the thigh. Her veins throbbed. Her skin felt itchy and tight.

Halfway through the presentation, Melanie walked in—pantsuit, chignon, heels clipping the linoleum. The teacher paused. Kevin cleared space and waved like a child to a parent from the stage of a school play.

Poor guy. Skylar arches, points her shoulders down and back toward him. Truth is, Melanie never would have farmed off Kevin if she thought someone else might want him. Sweat gathers on his brow. He presses Skylar's nipple like an elevator button. Presses it again, with renewed curiosity, as if he's never seen such a beastly thing. He takes it between his fingers and twists. Milk shoots him in the eye and they snort, they actually snort, with laughter. Her body hums. If Melanie commanded respect, Skylar radiated sex. She is pure animal instinct. She can't walk down the street without dogs trailing her, rising onto hindquarters to shove their wet noses into her legs, undeterred by strollers and slings; she is mounted and humped before the light changes, crossing the street and taken by surprise but she doesn't mind, her face flushed in the knowing reflections of pet owners, but otherwise she feels no shame. This is who she is—who we all are essentially—and she is obliged for the reminder. If nothing else, she is not yet dead.

"Are you Luke's mom?" Kevin had said weeks later at pick-up, explaining that Skylar's son was all their little Ralph talked about. Luke and his magnetic tiles. Luke at the sensory table. Luke with his soon-to-be baby sister. They went for coffee. It was refreshing that Kevin wasn't a mother. Playdates began. Kevin picked the boys up and took them to the park, for pizza. Sometimes Skylar tagged along but Kevin could handle it solo. He was a seasoned parent, with another child in fifth grade and a pair of teens from a previous marriage, in college, rarely mentioned, Skylar assumed, for the sake of Melanie. Skylar was grateful for his expertise.

"How can I repay the favor?" she said, when Kevin brought home Luke, fed and bathed and sleepy.

"Don't mention it," Kevin said. "It's entirely my pleasure."

He lifts her breast to his mouth. Her ducts release. Milk rushes from her. She is a faucet. His Adam's apple works overtime as he swallows. She is that much.

"Yum," he pops up and winks.

There is a white droplet by his eye, like a tear. Once Doug squeezed her into his coffee, just to taste, then returned to black. Skylar knows there are pockets on the Internet devoted to adult breastfeeding— there are pockets devoted to everything—though she cannot picture Kevin and Melanie populating these circles. She unpins her legs. Kevin dips between them. She could come right there. She could come without any further touch, like that first time in high school science class, which took her by surprise, like biting into the center of a Chewel's. She feels woozy, as if she's both drunk and high. Kevin has been drinking since lunch on the slopes and has kept on steadily through evening. She's noticed he is never completely blitzed but also never sober, a steady happy hour Claus. Skylar can taste tannin on her lips, or maybe that's the pot, stronger than she remembered, igniting her nerve endings. She is a live wire thanks to Kevin's enthusiasm, his tongue in relentless pursuit, as if trying to recapture his own adolescence, pushing through her like a brick of flat nails, a gift shop toy she's shoplifted, she wants to take the money and run, she lifts her hips, she almost has it, a little to the left, ready, right there, she is selfish and greedy and driven by need, an insatiable itch, but wait, not yet, hold everything, hold up.

Emma wails from the crib. Skylar leaps to soothe, but Kevin intercepts her efforts, his belly full, his pelvis pressing as he lifts her in his apelike arms. Her legs pedal the air as he carries her back to the couch, where he hovers, his body bridged over hers. They stay like that, Skylar on elbows until the baby stills and Kevin slides to his knees, his mouth lapping at the stream, catching what she spills, trembling beneath the torrent she has become: a pump, a fountain, an endless well, nothing is keeping her back anymore so she lets go, the convulsions fast and long, a salt lick flushing her wounds.

He can't squiggle his pants off fast enough.

"I can't believe this is happening," he says, with all the wonder of Peter Pan. *What is there to believe?*

"Oh sweet momma," he moans. She shuts her eyes. Her stomach churns. Animals were lucky, spared of talk, of mood lighting and consequences and lingerie. She palms his chest and eases out from under him, pushing her way in front. On all fours, she braces herself against the couch. His balls smack her ass. She breathes, he breathes. He is more or less the same as Doug, slightly thicker. They settle into a rhythm and for a minute it's so quiet she crawls right into it, back and forth, her focus is everything, she thinks she could come again until he roars, "Timber!" and collapses over her back like shot meat.

With that, it's over. Kevin sighs and rolls, immediately dreaming. His pants are bunched at his ankles. His manhood, a fraction of the size it once was. The fire on its way out. Slowly, so as to not disturb, Skylar rises and pees, then grabs a glass of water and stands in front of the kitchen window drinking, catching the outline of her face, the window hissing its drafty disapproval. She wraps a blanket around her shoulders but it provides no comfort from the wind. There is poor insulation. She can feel it from the inside. Outside, snow falls deep in the woods, silent yet furious. Kevin, Ralph and Luke, Emma, all peacefully sleeping. Skylar slips into her boots. Her phone pings. A text from her husband: *How's it going?* She opens the door. Winter rushes in. Before stepping out, she pulls a hood off the row of coat hooks. It is by itself, attached to nothing. Her phone vibrates again. She types: *Great. Love u. Sweet dreams.*

She remembers her father telling her mother all those years ago, "Heat escapes fastest through the head," how her golden hair shimmered in the cold, cold light. This hood is lined in fur, soft and gray, her own private animal. It's amazing, how warm it is, what a luxury, how well the head covering muffles sound. In the darkness she won't hear a thing.

CHARITY CASE

For all that she wants, Janie knows Mr. Neilson will never kiss her. He conducts. When he conducts, his hair whips, his arms fly through the air. His mustache glistens. There are dark rings in his pits. Janie wants to be the kind of person whose devotion yields dark rings. Her father calls this giving it one's all. Her mother gave it her all. She lost. There are no miracles. There are only days. Days marked by dinners from the coordinated meal chain. Days of ladies with Pyrex and tinfoil; pitying ladies who draw Janie to their stuffy breasts, to comfort their own worried hearts, to convince themselves that Janie's mother's fate won't befall them.

The neighborhood has seen enough. Janie has seen casseroles, stuffed shells. She saw one lady of the chain bent between her father's knees. Mr. Neilson, Janie heard, does not even like girls. He'd been a daytime soap star before becoming a music teacher, she heard; she's also heard about hamsters and celebrity buttholes. Janie knows you can't believe what you hear. On the gym bleachers, she stands next to Candace Connor whose mom supposedly had her at 15. They are both altos. Once, Janie saw Candace's mom at the roller rink in Jordache jeans. She is beautiful. Candace's mom will live forever.

Today is the dress rehearsal. They sing Rudolf, Frosty, Hallelujah. Mr. Neilson works himself into a froth for "Do You Hear What I Hear?" which is done in a round. Janie lip-syncs the Jesus parts of "Silent Night," and still her face reddens like a hot plate. Her voice is not missed. Mr. Neilson only accepted her into chorus because of her mother.

At the funeral, other mothers brought Janie gifts wrapped in silver and blue. Her father passed along these gestures of kindness; there was nothing to do but pass along other people's gestures, as if they might alleviate grief.

Every night of Hanukah he gave her a dollar bill "to put in a safe place." He gave her knee socks. Today, with the socks, she is wearing her jean skirt with the snaps and flare, a white button-down her father found in the boys' department. Her calves itch. She smells like apple juice. A meal chain lady tried to do something about her hair last night, but Janie said, "Thank you. You've done enough."

When they sing about dreidels, Mr. Neilson gives Janie an extra head bob, which makes her cheeks burn. She's not sure if she should feel special or singled out. Chorus is supposed to make her feel less alone. Tomorrow, they'll go downtown as a group to Wanamaker's. They will do their show in the department store lobby between cosmetics and perfume. The lobby will be festooned in lights and pine and poinsettia. They will sing, and the shoppers and salesclerks and non-working parents will whoop and clap. Afterward, every child in Brook Valley District Choir will ride the escalator to the North Pole.

The gate will be strewn in clumps of fake snow, like the inside of quilts. In his chair, Santa will be flanked by candy canes and human elves. For balance, there will be a cardboard oilcan. It will look like a genie's lamp. There will also be electric menorahs, whose fat orange bulbs will either be lit wrong or burned out. Not that it matters. The holiday falls differently each year. This year, it is already over.

In "Joy to the World," Janie makes perfect O's with her mouth, like Mr. Neilson taught her. She wonders if he notices. She wonders what the ladies will bring for dinner tonight, when they'll stop bringing; when the ladies will be replaced by just one lady. She wonders how she'll respond to Santa tomorrow, if she'll be fresh or demure, if she'll deliver a laundry list. Last year she wore her Star of David defiantly on his lap, only instead of dismissing her, he tightened his grip, and said, "Jewish girls can want things, too."

GOD'S CHILDREN

I met Lillian in August.

Her family moved in next door in late spring, but even those that trumpet their southern hospitality don't dream of turning on the oven for a friendly pie, much less leaving their air conditioning to inquire after new neighbors. The entire city holes up in the Texas heat. There isn't much I trumpet.

I was wrestling Max from his car seat and groceries from the back when she tapped me: damp swimsuit, cherry ice mustache, hand on the beach towel cinched to straight hips.

"Need help?" she said and wrung out her hair. It was long and shiny as eggplant skin. Her bangs were homemade. The water plinked onto the pavement. She stuck her finger in her ear and squeaked it around, then extended it toward me.

"Leave go," she said, tugging at a bag in my elbow.

I relented, readjusting my load. I shifted Max higher up on my hip and pried his grip from my hair.

"I can take it," she said, going for a box of diapers. She was doing this hopping thing with full arms and no shoes. Painted hearts leapt from her toes. I urged her off the pavement but she said it toughened her calluses, so I nodded in the direction of my apartment and up we went.

At the landing, she dropped the packages and retrieved the glasses that had been tucked into the neckline of her swimsuit. The frames were purple tortoiseshell; immediately, the lenses fogged. Her irises bloomed. She told me her name was Lillian.

"What a beautiful, grownup name."

"I'm not named for anyone special."

I told her that didn't detract from its loveliness.

"Because I am adopted," she said. "We came from McKinney."

I'd remembered the truck, the movers hauling bedspreads and wicker up the wrought iron staircase to her apartment, bandanas blooming from dungarees.

"Y'all aren't from around here," she said.

"My husband is," I said. "Born and bred."

"What's with the box?" She tapped the mezuzah on the doorpost so I explained it was a Jewish thing and she said, That's OK, as if she were accepting an apology.

"My uncle once worked for a Jewish." She wanted to know if I was a real strong one. I wasn't sure what she meant, so she told me how once her family tried to keep the Sabbath for Jesus's sake, but how hard she found it, what with the rules against electricity and Saturday morning cartoons, with the stores here being closed on Sundays, besides.

"When do you find time to shop?"

I said I wasn't that strong of a Jew.

"I'm 11 almost 12, but I bet you thought I was older, everyone does, on account of how I conduct myself. How old is he?"

Max razzed in her face.

"Eleven months."

"Is he adopted?"

I shook my head, plopped down Max on the welcome mat.

"Me and my brother and sister are all adopted only not from the same family, so we couldn't be more different. Why isn't he adopted?" she said, meaning Max, sitting like a blob. "You didn't want to adopt?"

"He just sort of came along."

"Didn't you want him?"

I looked at Max rocking himself on the jute. He had his fist in his mouth and his shirt was soaked in drool.

"My mom wanted us so bad she prayed for us," Lillian said.

I said how nice to be wanted like that.

"My mom, that is, not my *mom*."

Lillian crouched before Max and brushed the curls from his forehead. He stretched his stubby fingers toward her round face.

"When I turn 18 I can't wait to adopt. I'm going to be Angelina Jolie!" With that, she sprang up and raced down the steps and across the driveway and up the stone path to her own place.

"Thanks for the hand," I called. The screen door swung behind her.

A few weeks later, I saw her in the playground. It was early on a Saturday so people were out walking their dogs or squeezing in a jog or airing out their kids on the jungle gym. Lillian abandoned her scooter in a mulch heap beside the swings. She was wearing a frayed denim miniskirt and sneakers without socks. Her laces, untied, looked like rattails. Her training bra pressed through her T-shirt like a rubbing. An iPod hung from her neck.

"Hi," she said. She flipped her hair. "Hello, Max-a-million."

Max called her Dada.

Lillian asked to hold him, so I untangled him from the seat basket and handed him over and she grimaced, so I pointed to a park bench and down we sat.

"He's heavier than my dog, Roxie," she said, passing Max off so she could wriggle into her pocket for a wallet-sized photo of a beagle with a pink rhinestone collar. "She lives at my dad's so I see her on weekends."

I complimented Lillian on her dog and Max swiped at it so she told him to quit it. His diaper stank. How long had it been? I measured time in feed, poo, sleep, baby music class eternity. She sat there massaging the image with her thumbs. The gloss smudged. I thought of the heartthrob posters I taped to my childhood bedroom. Where was Matt Dillon now? She pushed her frames to her nose.

"My dad lets me stay up for *Desperate Housewives*."

I said how nice and she swung her dusty shins.

"Don't tell, but I started shaving."

I said her secret was safe and she said, "Even down there."

Max dove for her, so she took him back and bounced him on her knees, his body solid as a bag of sugar. Lillian kissed his nose and he opened his mouth.

"Down boy," she said.

"He likes you."

"Max, max, bo bax," she sang and he loved it.

"Banana fanna fo fax," she sang and he loved it some more so she bounced, "Me my mo max," and he threw up all over her.

"What the freckles?"

I tried to explain. Some babies, like Max, were just pukers.

"That's nasty," she said and dumped him on me.

Lillian was mopping her skirt with a wipe when this other kid showed up and cast his dim shadow over her. A hayfield of hair swooped over his eyes.

"Lilly, we've got to go."

"This is my brother, Colton," she said, kept wiping.

He said, How do you do, in a nervous way, eyes measuring the ground. He was working a laser pen in his shorts pocket. The red light blinked like a signal.

"He's older than me, but you'd never know it."

I asked Colton how old he was and he said, 13.

"Girls mature faster," Lillian said.

"Mom's waiting."

"Like I care." She didn't budge. Colton flashed his pen through his khakis again so I said, neat pen.

"Bought it at CVS." He interrogated my eyes like a roadside officer.

"Colton's adopted too," Lillian said.

"From extraterrestrials," Colton said.

"You wouldn't know we were related." She slid off the bench. "But that goes for you and Max, too. Doesn't he look like anybody?"

I said she should see the mailman and she said what for, and Colton pleaded once more in his nervous way and then a white SUV pulled up. There was a wreath stuck to the grill left over from Christmas. The window opened. In the front seat slouched a teenager in a tank dress. Her shoulders stuck out like lonely hills. The driver stretched across the passenger side.

"Come on, Lily-Ann, we're going to be late!" the woman called, sunglasses atop hair, so I took her for the mother.

"IN A MINUTE!" Lillian's face steamed. "Don't be rude! Can't you see I'm talking to my friend? She's a Jewish!"

The mother shot me a glance, like the one Joe's aunt gave me that first Easter, before countering, "I don't care if she's French Canadian, get your rear end into this car or you're not going to your father's next weekend!"

At this, Lillian burst into tears and Colton mumbled, "Told you," and my face burned as I plugged Max's mouth with a pacifier.

"You're so unfair!" Lillian shrieked; "unlike *you*," she said, misting her pancake breath all over my neck then taking off in the opposite direction.

"I'm counting to ten!" her mother said as Lillian fled. Colton picked up her scooter and lugged it to the car, the metal frame clanking against his calf, leaving it to the teenage passenger to bust out the door and tackle Lilly with her shoulders.

"Pardon us," Lilly's mother said.

I nodded. Max ripped out his pacifier and shoved it up my nose.

The girls returned from the field, staggering like drunks.

"Hell raiser," the older one said, plucking grass from Lilly's hair.

"Devil spawn," Lillian said, tugging at the awkward hem of that dress. It didn't improve the fit any.

Eleanor was the sister. She was skateboarding on the sidewalk when I saw her: Ski cap on Labor Day, boxy jeans, high-top sneakers with the logos hacked out of them. I asked why she wasn't at the town pool, and she said there was more to life than splashing around like a goddamn moron. I couldn't imagine what in hundred-degree heat, and she told me she was reading Plato and John Stuart Mill. She had to shout this because a team of gardeners had hitched up their *Ghostbusters* packs and had begun blowing leaves from the sidewalk.

"I've almost completed the entire syllabus for AP philosophy," she shouted over the din. She'd just started her freshman year at the local high school. I knew this school was top notch—Joe's alma mater—but I didn't remember any kind of AP philosophy back when I was in school, much less freshmen being eligible.

"Times have really changed," I said.

"No shit, Sherlock."

I watched her destroy a pimple.

"Bet you didn't think I'm a brainiac." She snapped her board. "Wear black in this town and people assume you're wrong in the head."

I said just maybe not in this weather, which didn't amuse her, so I assured her I didn't hold any preconceptions about her intellect.

"I'm no Satan worshipper, either."

I agreed that made two of us.

"Actually, I'm blessed." Her younger siblings were being home-schooled while their mother was between jobs, which explained why I'd often seen Lilly and Colton sneaking video games on the library desktops or grabbing an ice cream from the strip during school hours, slinking off with bouquets of taster spoons, which didn't seem all that unfortunate.

"They're not quite fit for the classroom, is how my mother puts it. Lilly has her temper and Colton sees his letters backwards and upside down. They call me the smart one, not to compare. We're all God's children."

Tomorrow was homecoming. It seemed early in the season, but then I was a Yankee, 15 years out of high school, and football, I'd come to learn, was a very big deal in North Texas. Storefronts were frosted white and blue, team calendars in the windows. I asked her if that was why all the houses in the neighborhood had been dolled up in toilet paper.

"It's so John Hughes."

She looked at me blankly.

Papering was just something kids did without anything better to do, Eleanor explained. "Like cow tipping. For the boor-zhwah-ZEE."

I said the parents must get pissed about the cleanup and she looked at me like I was a parent myself, which fine, just not one of *them*, so I said, I mean, look at the care of their lawns, and she agreed it was pretty messed up how people exploited entire Mexican villages to clip their hedges and string their Christmas lights and we went back to being cool.

I asked if there was a homecoming dance and she said yeah, only she didn't know if she would take Brett Joseph or Avril McKay and then asked if she could borrow my car. Sure, I said. I wanted her to like me. I nodded at the curb where my hatchback stood with its gnat-splattered windshield and out-of-state plates, milk stench ripening in the sun, then wondered if I should clear it with her mom first.

"Forget it," she said.

I offered to give her a lift but she said that wasn't it. I could hear the disappointment in her voice, but also the resignation, as if she was used to people going back on their word.

"I mean it," I pushed. I said it's on my way. *Where was I going?*

"You don't understand."

True. I understood nothing. My shorts were streaked with mashed peas.

"No offense," she softened.

Colton popped out the front door.

"Ready?" Eleanor asked and Colton slid down the banister. Eleanor flipped her board, scratched her ankle with her shoe, and took note of Max sitting plump in his stroller.

"Is he walking yet?"

"Almost."

She said, "Just you wait."

The night the storms swept through North Texas, Lillian showed up at our door. Thunder I was used to, but flash floods and tornado sirens and ambushes of hail added new fear to the weather. I missed home, the regular turn of seasons. There was so much I missed. The electricity had blown, so Joe and I were fumbling in the cupboards for dinner.

"I've been ringing the bell." Lillian shivered, soaked in her jellies. "Guess that's out, too."

She'd come for a lighter. I led her to the kitchen, where we'd gathered our stash of candles and flashlights. Joe was manning the pasta.

"You're Max's father."

"So I'm told," Joe said.

Lilly sunk into a chair. I brought over a towel and socks. Her toes looked like raw squid. From the pocket of her windbreaker she removed a stuffed baby lamb. The coat was matted gray and starting to pill. She brushed the loose tobacco from its fleece and placed it on Max's highchair. His lip trembled.

She pranced the sad-looking thing across his tray and Max cried.

"Ba-a-a-a," she cooed and he batted the thing wildly.

"What gives?"

"It's the hour," I said.

"Always a mystery," Joe said.

"Aren't you, like, his parents?"

Max hurled the animal to the floor.

Lilly frowned. "It was my favorite. I thought he'd want it."

I picked it up and returned it, said the thought's what counts.

Max howled.

Joe opened a jar of sauce.

"Do you smoke?" Lillian asked. No, we said, which was mostly true.

"But you have a lighter."

Joe said precisely for such occasions.

"Do you mind?" she asked, fishing out a withered cigarette. I wanted to say, *Does your mother?* Instead I told her, not around the baby. She skulked off. The flint glowed alone in the next room.

We had a radio on battery in the kitchen. "Captain Jack" came on and Max grew quiet, so I belted out the chorus with a wooden spoon. Joe spiked a brow like *this is a bold version of you*. It was twister weather. What else was there to do? Lilly asked who the artist was and Joe said, "This old guy you've probably never heard of," and in a single look we went right back to the worn people we'd become.

"Bob Dylan?" she asked.

"Billy Joel," Joe said. Lilly said she totally knew him.

"He's a Christian, right?"

"Who's a what?" Joe said.

"Billy Joe?"

"Billy Joel?"

"That's what I said. Is he a Christian?"

I said it was doubtful.

"Could be," Joe said.

I mouthed the lyrics to Joe: *Your sister's gone out. She's on a date.*

He mouthed back: *You just sit at home. And—*

"Thought so," Lilly said.

"Either way, he doesn't make Christian music," I clarified and she said, that's the only music they're allowed to hear in her house, so I cranked it up and gave her a spoon and she slid barefoot along our floor and we laughed, surprising ourselves.

"Move over Tom Cruise!" I exclaimed.

"If you say so." She shrugged.

Joe opened a bottle and poured. I offered Lilly grape juice in a Kiddush cup and drizzled some into Max's sippy and we all clinked cheers, including Max. I even recited the blessing for wine but it didn't go over. Lilly swirled the dark juice suspiciously.

"Seriously," she said, putting down her glass. "Y'all have Coke?"

I shook my head and handed her a plate of spaghetti and we all tucked into the table and ate.

Over dinner Lilly said, "At my dad's we drink Coke with breakfast. Last weekend we went through a case—that's 24 cans—in less than two days. And you know what he did? Drove to the Tom Thumb for another 24."

Joe said he sounded like some dad.

I asked where her siblings were tonight and she said church.

"What about you?" I asked.

"What *about* me?" Lilly snapped.

We propped our feet on the table and popped truffles from Joe's boss, except for Max who slipped his hand into his pants while chugging a bottle. Soon the lights switched on, which was a good thing, as Max's diaper dipped to his knees and it was getting on bath time. I spread him out on the changing table and Lilly asked if she could undress him. Lillian pinched his fat rolls and Max tugged at himself then peed all over her. I grabbed a fresh shirt and gave her privacy to change. Joe ran the bath. There were dishes.

Colton showed up.

"Is Lilly here?"

He stood there like a drowned rat until Lillian appeared wearing a shirt that read, *Tie Me Up, Cowboy*. It swallowed her shorts so she looked naked underneath. Joe had bought it as a spicy way of announcing we were moving back to his hometown. There had been no discussion. It was not the shirt I'd chosen for her.

Lilly yanked Colton inside.

"They have truffles which is just like chocolate only specialer," she gushed, her tan arm stark against his pale neck.

I held a used sponge, food trapped in the wool.

"Catch," Lilly said, chucking her peed-on shirt at my head. Before I could protest, she called me rad. She said I had rad clothes.

"Like a *real* big sister."

"Mi closet es tu closet." I beamed.

Max crawled into the room in his duck pajamas. I lifted him and kissed him and he broke free and dove to the floor, shrieking. Joe gave Max a high-five then disappeared to his office, so I tossed the remote to the kids and left them in front of *So You Think You Can Dance*.

Every night Max and I sat in the dark for hours. We read books and I nursed him until he zonked out and slipped off me, mouth gumming the air. Whenever he woke, I repeated the routine. I didn't mind. In the quiet, I didn't have to explain myself. Soon enough, Max would grow up, go to sleep by himself, leave home for college—but Joe said I ought to mind. It wasn't healthy. I was not just a mother but a wife. What about *him*?

Tonight during tuck in, I felt harried, self-conscious. I could hear the dryer tumble and whir. I could hear the kids in the living room. Eleanor had joined them on the couch. I never asked her about the homecoming dance, whom she wound up taking, or what was up with the sweat bands on her wrists, was it fashion or a plea for help. I didn't say we all try to cover aspects of ourselves, or do you want to talk about it. On her lap was a drenched stack of flyers that read: JESUS.

"They're best when you suck them," she was saying, licking her thumb. Lillian snickered. Max started crying.

"He's learning to self-soothe." No one seemed to hear me.

"Mom's going to flip." Colton had that laser in his shorts again.

"Shut up and eat," Lilly said, reaching for the truffles.

"I mean it." Colton's light winking. On, off, on.

"There was a power outage," Lilly said.

"An act of God," Eleanor said.

"We should go," Colton says. "Before she loses it."

"Who?" Eleanor said with a mouthful.

"Mom, stupid! Mom! Mom! Mom!"

Max's wails escalated. Crib bars shook. I felt sick. "Sleep experts claim it's best to let them figure it out by themselves."

"She isn't coming," Lilly said.

"Funny! Har-Har! Like I haven't heard that one before!" Colton said, but I could see the veins in his neck. He took out his laser and rolled it between his palms.

My whole body ached. I pictured Max sailing animals onto the floor, chin wet, a goopy mess.

"Seven out of ten marriages won't survive the first year of parenting," I said, digging half-moons into my palms. I could hear him sputtering tears, rattling the bars.

"I didn't leave a note," Eleanor said in the shadows.

Colton looked up. "You didn't."

"Have faith." Lilly crossed her arms.

"We're officially missing."

"Are not," Colton said.

"We're on our own."

"Always were. Always will be."

My son began to vomit.

"She should do something about that," Eleanor said.

"Is he possessed?" Colton said.

Lilly waved them off. "Some babies are just like that."

Tears ran hot, clouding my vision. Throughout sleep training, we'd gotten this far but no farther. I cupped my ears as he wretched. It sounded like an exorcism. The living room spun and spun. Ours was a world that taught us to ignore children. As if that built character. As if neglect led to resiliency later in life.

"Where were we?" Joe came up beside me.

"Your shirt's dry," I said to Lillian.

The child turned to me. "Great," she said. "We could really use some Coke."

LET ALL RESTLESS CREATURES GO

In June I enrolled in Ocean County Community College. It cost practically nothing if you lived instate and I was tired of being shut-in, like some ogre in a cave. I was tired of our sad house and its smell of forgotten bathwater. I was 19. What was life, anyway? When I told my father I was going, he winced as if the shock were physical, then recovered with a blessing and a brisk hug, chins over shoulders, careful not to touch too much, lest we catch each other's shortcomings.

My father's sister, Lena, and her husband, Mark, had a place in Waretown, so in exchange for laying their laminate flooring they let me crash. Their house was a ten-minute drive to campus, and they'd just installed a shower in their basement, a toilet next to the boiler, so I had to piss sideways in order not to burn myself. I slept on a futon and brushed my teeth in the laundry sink, but Mark stocked the mini-fridge and Lena radiated eagerness like an electric heat, like she was auditioning for the role of her life, running off to Kohl's with fresh purpose, returning with mouthwash and flashy boxes of tissues, even though I hadn't asked for anything.

I registered for Korean I, Business Management, and Wetlands Ecology. I was a first degree black belt and a fledging handyman, but the third course, billed as a cross between environmental science, of which I knew little, and marine biology, of which I knew less, was the one that had me stoked. Suddenly, it seemed possible to learn beyond the rote memorization necessary for my GED. Lena said I might as well take advantage of the coastal offerings. She said this as if by coastal she meant worldly, and she was right; if I wasn't willing to lean into new experiences, I might as well go back to Bergen County.

The first day, I was nervous. I wasn't used to school, to other people. Lena bought me a Jansport, brushed suede, which I filled with random crap so it wouldn't hang off me loose. We stood in the kitchen waiting on coffee. She'd just come off her shift—she was a physician's assistant at Barnabas Health—and her faded green scrubs were splashed in iodine. There was a kink in her forehead from her surgical cap. The smell of latex rose off of her. She stuffed a banana into a brown bag.

"In case you get hungry, Nick."

Lena smiled the smile I imagined she offered patients with chronic, indeterminate pain. I stared at the thing. I couldn't remember the last time I had a banana that wasn't in deli chip form.

"To fresh fruits," she said. We clinked mugs. My aunt wore her wedding ring like a charm around her neck, the skin above her breasts flushed with freckles. I wasn't looking on purpose; I just wasn't big on eye contact, and there they were: spilling over with kindness. They looked like a burden. Lena peered beneath the brim of my hat.

"Go get 'em," she said, then rustled my head. My hand flew up and she retracted hers as if stung as the air whooshed over my bare, naked scalp.

On my eleventh birthday I started losing my hair. It began slowly, a change purse of spots, symmetrical rounds the size of dimes, nickels, silver dollars. A fist of hair in the shower, a clutch in a comb, odd clumps on my pillow like some kind of furry present, the color once blonde now sandy, indistinct, shit brown.

"What have you done to yourself?" my father said.

"Nothing." I lowered my spoon into my breakfast cereal.

"You think she'll return for a freak?"

My mom had been gone two years; she traveled with the New York Philharmonic, so it's not like she was dead, only busy. She had a studio apartment in Lincoln Center, but as the principal cellist she was in constant demand. There was always some place to be. My father did not push. This is not who we were. Mothers, newts, lightning bugs, we were not trappers, we did not hold anything against their will, but opened our hands to the moonlit sky, let all the restless creatures go.

Later, he'd take back the name-calling. My father never meant harm. It was an honest mistake. The patches looked deliberate, as if I'd used razors and scissors to transform my head into a chessboard, as if I was asking for it, setting myself up for ridicule, begging for attention. I assured him visibility was the last thing I wanted. He suggested dark colors. He said, Sit in the back row. We didn't say more about it until Vinnie Frankel called me grandpa and tripped me on the stairs, giving me a fat lip. The guidance counselor said I should see someone. A few weeks later a specialist performed the full work-up: blood, piss. My glands were neither hypo nor hyper. The bad news and the good: I was a normal kid. She gave me some topical creams and shrugged. There were no real drugs to prescribe. Premature hair loss fell into the lumpy, amorphous category of auto-immune disorders. It's not like I could plant some seeds and water myself, add direct sunlight and await bloom.

"There's little you can do," the doctor said, scribbling on a pad. "Try to eliminate stressors in your life." I wasn't stressed. I played video games. School was school. My dad worked, came home. We ate. Washed the dishes. My mother called from Vienna, from Budapest. The phone rang and rang but we no longer leapt up to answer.

I wasn't stupid. I wore headphones to block out the teasing and enrolled in martial arts, mastering my 360 roundhouse kicks until I'd climbed the ranks from green belt to brown to red. Sometimes I stayed late to clean the mats, and Sensei Will would buy me a soda and tell me about anime, those big eyes and tits. Once he took me to a cosplay convention in a hotel lobby where people paraded around signing autographs as if they really *were* the stars they pretended to be. He coughed up 30 dollars for a selfie with a throng of girls in roller skates and crop tops. They were all playing the same character. I didn't get it.

"What is there to *get*?" Will snapped.

That was the end of tae-kwon-do.

"Dude," Will said, tying my black belt for the first and last time. "Do yourself a favor. Don't try to be a hero. Wear a goddamn hat."

Wetlands Ecology met on the third floor of the Marine Life building, a concrete structure the color of wet sand. The room was large and overly air-conditioned, little swingy desks in a circle, the students, a mix of young and old, tapping on their phones. I sat by the window and waited. Outside, people walked along the campus path, their backpacks bobbing behind them like buoys.

"Are we in the right place?" Professor Jay announced, arriving in a fluster of papers. She wore nylon cargos and a plaid button down tucked into a nautical weave belt; plopped everything down on the desk. She could have been 50 or 70. When she turned, her long silver braid swished like a satisfied tail. She wrote her name and number on the board.

"This is where to find me."

No one wrote it down.

From there, she laid out course procedure. No tests, no grades. This would be the only time we'd meet in the classroom. Diamondback terrapins were decreasing dramatically. In some states they were already endangered. Our mission was to save what remained. She produced a laminated fact-sheet with a photo of the native New Jersey turtle, neck stretched pencil-dick thin, its shell a patchwork of yellow and green. We were in the height of mating season.

"It's now or never," she said. From here on, we were to think like scientists and act like human beings. All fieldwork would be conducted from the protected terrapin hatchery down in Barnegat Bay. As she said this, she passed around a sign-up sheet. One column if you had a car, another if you needed a ride. We'd be matched together accordingly.

"Objections?"

"Or forever hold your peace," drawled a girl from the back. Her springy hair fell past her shoulders, one side shaved by the ear. She wore a purple tank, wide upper arms meant for decking and lugging weight. She knifed two fingers in the air.

"Well, then." Professor Jay clasped her hands. "Let's begin."

No one could explain why it was happening, why it happened to me. If there was a genetic link to hair loss, it skipped every other generation. The doctor clicked her pen. "Alopecia totalis," she said with a superior uptick, as if the diagnosis was rocketry science. My condition sounded like a drug for erectile dysfunction, a loving couple of senior citizens skyward in a hot air balloon. She left the room. A nurse returned with brochures. Options, she said. She lowered her voice. She knew a guy who made beautiful wigs, real natural looking.

Just say the word. She'd get me a good price. I dangled my legs off the edge of the examination table. My feet had jumped three sizes. They looked like swollen fish. She mentioned support groups for kids like me, handed over a pamphlet of the annual *Alopeciapallooza*: a sweaty, throbbing mob of bald teens.

My father buttoned and unbuttoned his coat, his fingers working the holes, twisting his wedding ring, running through his hair. Bushy at the sides, appropriately thin on top. He paced, circling a drain. I was his only child. "Thank you. We'll consult with his mother and get back to you." Only we never told her. There was no plan. No more doctors.

Because I had a pickup, I had room in the cab for one passenger. The girl in purple: Sahara Rain. I wanted to tell her she sounded like body wash or shampoo, but I couldn't remember the last time I was this close to another person. My stomach rumbled; that morning, neither Lena nor Mark showed up for breakfast so I left without eating. I hoped Sahara couldn't hear the sounds of myself. She smelled like bathroom spray, floral concentrate. I asked her to fasten her seatbelt. She asked to play DJ.

"Whatever you want," I said.

Before we pulled out, Professor Jay tapped on my window. I rolled down the glass and she nosed into the cab like a periscope. I wasn't sure where to look. Sahara's bracelets jangled.

"Give me a hand with supplies?"

I hopped out. We loaded up my flat bed with buckets, chicken wire, test tubes, pliers and pincers, lumber.

"Environmental science major?"

"Undecided." I'd been in school for all of five minutes.

"I can always sniff out those with grit."

I slammed the trunk.

"Don't be ashamed," Professor Jay said. "The perseverant are a rare and beautiful breed."

In the cab, Sahara fiddled with the dial. She had terrible taste, which wasn't entirely her fault. We were in the no-man's land between stations, all crackle and fuzz. I rolled down the window while she checked the traffic. It was sunny and hot, coming on a holiday week-end, and the Garden State was backed up in an oily haze. She stuck her phone in my face: an endless artery of red.

"We're not supposed to separate from the group."

"Screw that." She knew a better way on back roads, past aban-doned farm stands deep through the Pine Barrens. We made great time. When we approached the causeway, she cranked her window, the truck rattling in the wind. She unclipped her hair, thick curls frosted in strawberry and gold, and let them whip. She whooped like a wild thing. Her face reddened. She thundered her feet on my floor maps.

"Your turn, Saint Nick," she said. "Load and explode."

I gripped the wheel.

"I'm cool."

"And I'm endangered," she half-snorted, stretching her legs on the dash. A shaky vine inked her ankle. Birds cawed. Salt filled the air. The truck swayed like a drunk as I floored it to the other side.

We were the first to arrive in Barnegat Bay. Sahara climbed onto the hood, smacked the paint beside her.

"Sit," she said. Our thighs touched, our smells swirled, like we'd known each other forever. Like it was no big thing for her to look me in the eye and call me, "Baldy." To flop her mess of hair on my shoulder and say, "Tell me your sad story."

By high school I'd gone from totalis to universalis, thanks to the kamikaze nature of my eyelashes and eyebrows, the fuzz on my fore-arms diving off pier like despondent caterpillars. Once I was entirely hairless, I could relax. I'd already lost, nothing to do but adjust to my new normal. I was aerodynamic as a jet plane, a plucked chicken, Casper the Friendly Ghost, I was a load of laughs if I could take being the brunt of the joke. In the gym locker room, guys combed their armpits, measured their dark upper lips. I covered up: ball caps, truckers, newsboys. Rumors spread that I was sick, I was sickly, I lived in Ronald McDonald House. I did not correct them.

"Greetings, conservationists," Professor Jay said. We flocked around her. She climbed out of her car, a cream-colored VW bug, collaged in bumper stickers: FRACK OFF. SAVE THE BAY. EARTH FIRST. She shielded her eyes. "Is this all of us?" We numbered around 20, a handful having vanished after the first meeting. Sahara said that was typical. People came and went. This was her fourth term of classes at OCCC but she still was years away from any degree.

Jay charged into the wetlands and introduced us to its complex ecosystem, home to the osprey, gull, and egret. As she spoke, she removed the binoculars from her neck and circulated them. If we hoped to have any positive impact, we'd have to be tireless. Track the water's PH to gauge toxicity from the fumes at Oyster Creek, the nuclear plant whose concrete cylinders loomed in the distance, and which drew its cooling water from the estuary around which we stood. Recently, Jay reported, hairline leaks had been detected in the pipes but they were deemed too insignificant "to warrant a public health crisis." Jay pushed up her sleeves. "According to the EPA, this is the safest nuclear plant in the country, if you can swallow that oxymoron."

"Still, tritium bleeds. Still, no accountability. How much radiation can we take?" Her fist shook. I felt the class shift in my direction, the collective heat of their pity reminding me, lest I forget, that I looked like a chemo patient.

My face steamed.

Even Jay dealt me a nod. "Against all odds, we must fight. You are the future. You owe it to yourselves."

"Thought we owe it to the turtles," Sahara cut in.

That night, I joined my aunt and uncle for dinner. I was tired of subsisting on drive-thru hamburgers. I felt alive. I wanted to try to shape it, to tell Lena and Mark about class and Professor Jay, about Sahara Rain on the causeway waving in the wind. I wanted to say, I'm excited to be a part of something, something bigger than me, and I wanted Lena to draw me tight and say, You've got this, even if I wasn't 100% sure what *it* was. On my way home I'd pulled over at the ShopRite to pick up ingredients for mud pie, graham cracker crust and instant chocolate pudding, ready set without baking. This is what my father made for special occasions. I shook a festive can of whipped cream, only when I came upstairs Mark and Lena weren't feeling up for dessert. Lena picked at her lasagna. It looked like entrails. Her eyes were bloodshot. She didn't say a word. No one asked about my day. Mark stood in front of the sink. The faucet ran. He picked up a sponge and wrung it.

"It's not selfish." Mark spoke tightly, like he was trying to balance a toothpick in his jaw. "Just because other people do it is not a reason to follow." I tilted the canister, shot a cloud into my mouth. He said, "Nick, if everyone you knew jumped off a bridge, would you?"

I wiped my lip, swallowing the pillowy cream. "I don't know many people."

Mark said, "Bingo. Lena, I rest my case."

For 12 weeks, on Tuesdays and Thursdays, we drove. Sahara talked, starting with her morning alarm and taking it from there, filling the ride with her astrology reports, her rising sign, her sun and moon signs, speaking at the same clip regardless of whether she was detailing her struggles with English comp or her cat's diet or her brother's moody-ass girlfriend, a nasty drunk Sahara had to throw out of the bar where she worked because that was the thing about people, she said, they always turned out to be shitbags. It was a lot to take in, I couldn't follow it all, to tell the truth, I wasn't always interested, but sometimes I was, sometimes we even went back and forth a bit, her seat back, her skirts hitched up her thighs. Sometimes, she'd tap my arm, her nails filed to points, shooting sparks up my spine. On the causeway, we howled. She had this way of looking at me without looking at all, as if I wasn't some pale, bald mutant. As if I was just a guy.

The field site was serious business. We were there to work. A few people goofed off, kicked the dunes, cursing the sand in their eyes. Professor Jay snatched one kid's pack of cigarettes and told him to come back once he decided to stop trying to killing himself. The rest of us hunkered down. We got muddy. We waded calf-deep, minnows scattering, a stinging cold, and drew test samples of everything. One group took up shovels and metal poles and carried them like crosses through the salt grass, affixing road signs along the curb: yellow diamonds that said TURTLE CROSSING. As if raccoons and coyotes could read. Black stenciled prints of a mother and offspring accompanied the words CAUTION. BE TERRAPIN AWARE! The sign trussed with blinking reflectors. A second group was tasked with rebuilding the battered nesting station, damaged by winter. They dragged sheets of wire to reinforce the rescue. I wasn't sure how the eggs were going to get inside. Group 3 answered that question. They tiptoed around, crawled in gloves bright as toothpaste. It was their job to relocate the clutches of eggs to safety without crushing them. Sahara was in this group. As she combed the edges of the bay, I held my breath. I remembered the time my mother led me through the orchestra pit during a practice break, hands on belly, lest I collide with a music stand. Still, I managed to slam into a woodwind. Sahara presented her eggs like jewels. I counted their brown spots, tagged them, and tucked each into its own incubating compartment. I named them Eenie, Meenie, Miney. I named them Larry, Curly, Moe.

"What's the good word?" Professor Jay came over in waders and a ranger's hat. She took my hand. I thought she wanted an egg but instead she examined my palm, tracing each crease with a finger. Head line, life line, heart line. She smelled like eucalyptus. At first it was kind of nice, to be touched at all, but then, you know, *weird*. My egg train was backing up. Sahara was waiting, others behind her.

"Promising," Jay said.

I slipped my hand from her grip.

When I got home, Lena was at the kitchen table, fingers to temples, box of red wine dripping at the spigot. I backed out slowly but the door creaked. "I don't bite," she said. Lena offered me her glass, a fossil print of lipstick on the rim. I asked if she was okay.

"Why? Don't I seem happy?"

I said I wasn't sure what happy looked like.

"Sit down and humor me."

So I told Lena about school, class. How we'd salvaged 11 new eggs from predation, increasing their chance of immediate survival to 85%. Measured growth circumference with pincers and nestled them into the designated pockets we'd carved so we could monitor them in anticipation of next month's hatching. In a way intervention felt wrong, I said, to disturb their natural habitat, put our hands on everything, but Professor Jay said we'd already done enough injury, decimating the species by a quarter, that the least we could do with our short time on the planet was try to fix past mistakes, give the turtles every chance we could—just as we would our own children.

At that, Lena uttered a strained sound, like someone was squashing her.

I said I bet it was the same as her profession, the saving part.

"No one's a hero," she said. "Except maybe your father. My brother's a foolish saint." I didn't see it. All I could picture was his car in the driveway, the wood-paneled living room, heavy drapes. Home was a coffin but for his music, *The Umbrellas of Cherbourg* soundtrack tinkling on repeat. "He might not say it, but he misses you. He loves you more than life."

"I love it here," I said. "You and Mark rule. You're my family."

A sob escaped her. I think it surprised us both. I tried to comfort her but she wasn't having it. She placed her hand over mine.

"Just call him, okay?"

Sahara wanted to ditch. It was August and she was dying, dying of heat, she said. What about Jay? I said. What about me? Sahara said. I'd be cruel to refuse her a day at the beach. The island was so narrow, less than a half mile from ocean to bay, that it was a no-brainer. Hadn't we worked hard enough? Everyone deserves a reward. She slapped my arm. I flexed. I'd been lifting with Mark's free weights. Still, no way was I taking off my shirt. Sahara, on the other hand, had come ready in a bikini, her jet-black triangle top exposing moons of flesh. She wriggled out of her shorts. There was a ring through her bellybutton, charmed with a royal blue bead of the evil eye. Actually, I'm needed at home, I dithered, a lie, Lena was on overnight shift and Mark had gone to Atlantic City. I'd caught him sleeping on the couch the other morning. Sahara saw right through me. She lifted the hair off her neck revealing a lopsided rose. Did it hurt, I wanted to know.

"Tattoos. What do they feel like?"

"Numb after a while." Her sunscreen was coconut sweet. I rubbed her back and shoulders, her skin bumpy, but warm. She pulled away, popped the car door and dropped her sandals on the dunes. I followed. Like a child, she ran for the surf. The tide was coming in. She did not look back but sped up to meet it, palms pointed, and dove through the waves before they broke over her.

My father had news.

"Your mother is getting married," he said. To a conductor in Berlin. Or maybe she'd already married. He wasn't sure. Poor connection when they spoke, but he'd manage to glean a whole band of step-siblings, a grand terraced flat along the Spree. He puffed. "I've been meaning to call you," which summed up my father: always meaning, not doing. "Hold on, I have her email." I heard the click of a mouse. "She forwarded a Eurorail Pass. Your belated graduation gift."

We never told her I'd dropped out.

"Listen, Dad."

"This could be a real opportunity, Nick. Show her the man you've become."

I thought maybe Sahara would go with me. That next day in the car, when she was raging about her roommate who couldn't make rent but hoarded CBD, I asked what she knew of Europe.

"For real?" She wanted the hell out of Dodge, she told me. To prove it, she tackled me. I pulled over. I couldn't believe it was happening. My safety buckle dug into her leg as she panted like a dog fresh out of the crate. Her hair tickled my throat, my neck, chest. I nearly burst. Then she took off my hat and placed it on her head, brim backward. She palmed my scalp, round and smooth as an egg, and kissed it.

Fog socked the bay. Professor Jay studied her numbers. In the last few days, everything had changed. Count was down. A mother terrapin had been run over in the harbor alongside its hatchling. And now, half a dozen eggs previously accounted for were missing.

"What went wrong?" I asked.

"You tell me." Predators, forces of nature, theft, human error. Even devotion was fallible. Jay tapped her pencil, her anger a brick. And yet, there was resignation in her voice as she spoke. Her braid had loosened. The semester was almost over. There was little to do other than make peace with it.

"And what—accept defeat?"

She looked at me, weary.

"Not defeat, Nick. Nature."

On the ride home Sahara said, "Some people, you know? They always draw the short stick." She produced a sample-sized mois-turizer from her bag, massaged it over her hands, the cream pink as the inside of a shell. I asked what people. *Jay*. Didn't I know? Her husband had early onset dementia.

"The guy can hide his own Easter eggs."

Sahara talked like this all was common knowledge. His deterioration was a direct result of environmental exposure. Jay cared for doomed reptiles and nursed a grown man who'd forgotten how to wipe himself. Sahara checked her teeth in the mirror, sucked.

"Can you imagine a lonelier life?"

I wondered aloud how she knew all this. She reached for her lip gloss.

"Pay attention, Nick. I know more than you think."

By late August, the terrapins began to hatch. Shells scattered the bay like jigsaw pieces. On our last class we tallied the hatchlings. All things considered, we did OK. For every survivor there were three dead. Time was critical. Professor Jay hauled a large glass tank onto the sand, something fit for python, tossed us a couple red buckets. We filled it with salt marsh then ran up the dunes to the hatchery. Gently, we unearthed them, cradling their tiny bodies in our hands like talismans, to safeguard them from boating and cyclist hazards, from other unknown elements. That was it. Jay would bring the tank to the on-campus lab for further monitoring. But our job was done.

So was Sahara. I will never understand it. One day she was strolling across campus in her ripped jeans, eating an Italian sub on the steps, extra salt and sweet peppers, and then she was gone. I texted but never heard back, I called but always got that double ring, no machine, the signal that her line was occupied. I even joined Facebook, but when I typed in her name there was only a picture of a cat in sunglasses, the rest of her account protected, private, gone. I wasn't about to chase her. I knew better. I emailed my mother a selfie. She sent me an invite to her opening gala in Berlin.

She wrote, "What's with the getup? It's not Halloween, you know. Have your father take you shopping. Leave the latex skullcaps at home. We're all adults here."

Lena and Mark said I could stay as long as I wished. I repaired the dishwasher. I painted their office sea green. An adaptable color, if not quite the gloss they'd wanted. Lena worked more, to accumulate hours, in case she got pregnant again. My father started driving down on Sundays. It was nice. We'd never really known each other. Afterward, Mark and I sat on the porch. The weather already had turned crisp. Minutes went by without cars.

Mark said, "Isn't the world full enough?"

That October, I ran into Professor Jay on campus. She was frazzled as usual, cloth bags on each arm like a set of scales. I was talking to this girl in my statistics class when she tugged my sleeve.

"Nick!" She said, breathless. "Can I borrow you?"

I excused myself. Jay asked if I still had the truck, so I pulled it around to her lab. With a flash of schoolgirl enthusiasm she waved me in, and suddenly, I pictured her and my father on Thanksgiving, all of us squeezed around Mark and Lena's table with aluminum-wrapped yams, a buttery loaf of cornbread. There was no science to bringing people together. Still, you never know. I followed her inside. There must have been 50 terrapins in saltwater tanks. Jay switched on a light. Seventy-three, to be exact, she said. Carefully, we carried them out to my flatbed. Jay checked the pH, balanced the brine. Then, we tied down the cages and shut the tailgate and pulled the tarp up and around like we were tucking them in for the night.

"Will they be okay?"

"It's only a short distance."

When we approached the causeway, I rolled down my windows and blasted the radio. I pounded my boots and floored it, as if I'd forgotten myself. Jay looked over, brow raised, a glimmer in her eyes.

"Habit," I said. Wind rushed in. When my hat blew off, I let it lie.

A fresh crop of students awaited her. One looked a bit like Sahara, with the hair and sunglasses, but it wasn't her. Two guys in track pants trotted over and took hold of a tank; Jay and I took the other.

"Watch it!" She cried, water sloshing against the sides. Everyone leaned in as Jay lifted a diamondback, its shell a glossy white from the coating she'd applied, miniature limbs pedaling in the air, as if desperate for some kind of grounding.

"You first," Jay motioned for me. I submerged my arms in the tank, handing off the baby turtles to Jay, who passed them to her students, who carried them one by one to the water's edge. It was a somber march. Although they'd made it this far, from the hatchery to the lab and home again, to their successful release, the new generation still faced long-term threat along the coastline. These were the odds. It was important to have realistic expectations. Even in ideal conditions, there is no guarantee.

THERE'S A JOKE HERE
SOMEWHERE AND IT'S ON ME

I mistook the Catholic schoolgirls for friends until I learned my mom paid them 50 cents an hour to pick me up from elementary and walk me home, knee socks slouched and kilts rolled at the hip. Philomena and Therese brought hairspray, brought boys, brought cigarettes. They watched *Dancing on Air* from the bus station sized black and white in the kitchen while I broke ramen into melamine. When they raided the back cabinet for dusty pints of banana liquor—one called Blue Lagoon the hue of 2000 Flushes—Holly showed up on her bicycle with a bell shaped like Jesus. Holly switched the dial to Bob Ross and his happy little trees, but money went missing; from there it took little convincing: MTV watched me. I watched MTV. "Legs," "Hot for Teacher." Sometimes I'd remove the sleeve of condoms from my mother's nightstand and stretch them over the spout, plump and jellied, launch them from her bedroom window. We shared our driveway with a rabbi and his wife. The wife pinned her laundry to an outdoor rack, web bent like an antennae searching for signal, flaunted tablecloths and bloomers, big and white. One night, she knocked in cat-shaped glasses to report her asphalt findings. Held the splattered remains with tweezers to the light where they shimmered like molted skin. Did my mother know the child she was raising, who I was, the kind of person I'd be, left alone, exposed to elements, how I'd turn out if my mom wasn't careful? My soul was at risk. Someone should keep an eye out. The rabbi's wife offered her services. My mother said thank you very much. I was nine. By 11, Sally Sellers' family would practically adopt me. In 1984, I had Bruce Springsteen. I had *Dancing in the Dark*. I lay on my mother's bed, mandala print, drinking Coke from the liter, lips feathered in sour cream and onion. I watched Bruce bop to the beat, side to side, as if to an earlier era, his hand swinging, his hand reaching, his hand ticking toward Courteney Cox, a ruse, of course, but I believed, then. I believed in his glance, that moment—*hey baby*, the outstretched hand, the other wrist doing that little flip—that she had been plucked from anonymity, that a person could be found like that. It was the only happy ending I needed. I watched the denim hug his hips. His groin thrumming, teeth teasing out a bite from his bottom lip. Decades later, I'd learn his song was not about sex but depression, the two inextricably twined. Bruce would write about this. Demons haunt everyone, even rock stars. Sally's dad looked just like him: dark curls, hooked nose, more Jewish than Jersey, but Saturday mornings after sleepovers, sweaty from his runs, it was easy to conflate, easy to see his arms—cuffs rolled, veins pulsing like a through line—easy to feel his hand, the wink, ache pushing against muscle, tugging at bone as if to say take, save me, we who neither can be saved nor contained, fingers brushing fingers, step close and touch, easy to get swept in the song and dance, on the waxed kitchen floor, easy now, *quiet*, before everyone else wakes, easy to believe he moved just for me.

RUNNER'S PARADISE

I'm taking up running, I tell my husband at breakfast.

My husband smiles through his juice. Adam is always running and he is always smiling a kinetic mouthful of fenced whites. He wears spandex shorts and neon shirts of breathable fabric. His man smell rises off of him, benign, like a tea: sweet grassy armpit. Pulp clings to the sides of his glass, translucent half-moons. Lately, I swear, he's been bouncing.

"For real?" Adam kind of half-sings. It is easy to make fun of my life choices, but everyone is good at something. Mine just happens to be inertia. I make couch potatoes look spry. Despite this, he is careful to say, Do what you want. This is his answer to everything. Why make the bed when it just gets messed up anyway? Adam tousles my hair. I feel like a puppy. There is a twinkle in his eye. Go nuts, he says, get wild and crazy, and walks out of the room.

My first time out I dress wrong. Sweatpants and a turquoise fleece headband—I look like an 80s tween—but it's hard to know how many layers a person needs. The weather is raw, not quite spring. My nose drips. The light dulls, flat on the track, but the path itself is scenic, an even five miles rimmed in trees, hedges, a bubbling brook, man-made lake, plastic paddle boats beached on the shore. I hunch and kind of waddle, as if there is a fresh load diapered between my legs. Coffee bitters my throat. Runners whoosh past. From their pinched, determined brows you'd never guess they're aware they are going nowhere, that it's all one big circle. Running will not bring them closer to anything. Cattails flop over the road. My feet drag along the asphalt. I huff and puff and punk out before I cross the first mile.

Back home, I am red in the face, my heart throbbing through my skull. It hurts to breathe so I ragdoll my knees and try not to hurl.

"We can't all be," Adam says, like that's supposed to make me feel better. He has a shelf in the family room for his trophies and medals. Hardware, he calls them. He buffs and shines. "Adjust your expectations. You're not about to become someone new overnight."

"Who said anything about new?" I wheeze.

"Maybe yoga is more your speed," he says, rubbing my back as if to burp me; as if to coax a blue-bodied genie out of me, as if I have wishes left to give.

"Run with me?" I plead, blinking away the sting of salt tears.

A fortune cookie on New Year's Eve: Don't stop when you hit a rough patch. My son adds, In bed, and cracks up. The kid's 11. Speaking of bed, I say. But Benji insists on the Times Square broadcast. Who doesn't want Katy Perry in a rubber dress? My five-year-old shakes her hips like confetti. After the ball drops and we climb the stairs, Kylie and Benji to their rooms, I place the paper slip into a jar of resolutions, shut the lid.

Adam comes along for a run but ditches me before I queue up a playlist. I'm still trying to figure out how I'm feeling. Today's hits or British trance? We've gone maybe 300 feet. Can't help you! He waves over his shoulder. I watch him peel off. Calves popping, puddle-jumping stride, he runs upright, such posture, as if a cattle prod is pushing him along, branding his backside. He passes on the right. Slow pokes keep left. Dog walkers spread out on the peripheral lanes. No one waves or nods or makes eye contact. Occasionally, a runner swerves onto a side path. There must be a half-dozen of these capillary trails leading god knows where. My arms crank like a rusty toy. I watch Adam among the weekend warriors, the ultra-obsessed, wings inked on their ankles, the former fat boys with jiggly breasts, the pony-tailed packs, the barefoot disciples, and those in sneaker gloves. I watch him blend in and think how nice it must be. Eventually, he fades from view.

My speed is 15 minutes per mile. I scroll through an activity app. My active heart rate is 180. My distance is 1.3 miles. My phone cheers: *Way to go!* It posts my results on the Internet where strangers can add emojis: thumbs, poop, stars. At home, I microwave a frozen Indian burrito; scrape off the moist towel I'd wrapped around it. Little bits of paper stick to the dough. The chunks of potato are cold in the middle, the curry a mustard paste, but I finish it off in three quick bites.

On the porch, I sit and wait for Adam, smelling like cumin. An hour later he leaps up the block. Lost? I venture but he's too fired up to hear me. Hot damn! He howls. He punches the air. That was a good, hard, long one. He points to himself reflected in the front bay window, the cleft of his chin a glistening river, and says: You the man.

I take myself shopping. Adam wants me to be happy. Who hasn't bought into an idea of happiness? 80 dollars for jogging pants, another 50 for the matching top, bright purple with a built-in shelf bra that flattens me out like a dosa. The girls in the store look alike, I don't know who's a customer and who's a clerk, but everyone says to trust them. Our technology is revolutionary, they say. This outfit will change your life. I slide my credit card across the counter.

At the custom shoe store, I mount a treadmill at the behest of a flannel-shirted professional. I'm more of an outdoor terrain type, I say, but he insists on evaluating my style. What style? He reassures me, We provide this service to even our most seasoned runners, sticking nodes on my chest. No other retailer specializes in biomechanics. Sounds serious, I say. Run, he commands, the machine at a pie-sized incline. I worry I'm going to fall off. Pay attention or you'll break a bone, he says. We want to keep you intact. Are you an overpronator or underpronator? I tell him I don't know what I am. 200 dollars later, he's figured me out.

Back home around the table, we swap newspaper headlines.

Adam says: "Can you believe they still haven't found the plane?"

"One in three couples cheat," I cite a new study published by a dating company for the unfaithfully married. The company sounds like a preppy clothing label, which I guess is good branding. You never know exactly what's being sold. "Has to be foul play," he says. "An international flight disappearing in thin air? Implausible. Everyone leaves a trace." His glasses slip off his nose. I smack the paper with the back of my palm: an ad of a woman, faceless, hushed finger to her lips. When Adam isn't running or working, he loafs around in plaid pajamas, flannel robe and suede moccasin slippers stuffed with vegan shearling—gifts accumulated since the dawn of fatherhood. It seems to comprise the male uniform of a certain age, background, economic bracket. Adam loves that term, economic bracket, piles on the garb regardless of the seasons as if starring in his own syndicated sitcom.

"Some use fake names, others fix up their own spouses, form a horny daisy chain." I read on. "The site also doubles as an underground fertility clinic of sperm donors and surrogates, for couples struggling to conceive."

"I guess we'll never know the full story." He pushes up from the table, sheds his robe. "I'm going for a run."

While he's gone, I model my new clothes. I clip the tags. In the full length I study my butt, the pudge sucked in and sculpted into two balls like the kind Adam keeps on his desk for stress relief. My stomach bulges over the elastic waistband, but there is no hiding trouble spots once you've had kids. I stand back for perspective, as if that might bring me into sharper focus. I step close. I press my chin to the glass until my eyes cross.

Adam says: If you want something, go after it. I suit up. Before he wakes, I dart out to the track. Years ago it was dubbed Runner's Paradise and I am lucky, the five-mile trail is practically in my backyard. People drive from miles to park in the adjacent lot. I run alone. In the beginning, the exercise feels futile, like chasing my own tail. By the second week, I start to understand—the purpose lies in the pursuit. I set goals, draft a schedule. I tell myself: Reach. Each day, I go a little farther. Each day, it becomes a little less awful. My lungs are no longer shredded balloons; I can almost feel them pinken. I manage to hit 2 miles, 2.5. Classic rock pounds in my ears, only now it's broadcast on the Oldies station. I squint out the edges of my lids. How many of these joggers have I seen at the mall, shot-gunned beers with in shitty bars? It's not a big town and I've never left. Still here, I say, panting, until it becomes a mantra. Still here, I count the miles:

three, four, drenched in sweat. I feel better already. Still here, I grunt at the gravel and the squirrels, the nests of pine needles, until I am back where I started. Here. Still. I've made a full lap around.

My husband fogs up the shower. He shaves his chest, his legs. He is aerodynamic. "Faster than a speeding bullet!" Kylie lisps. Adam has trained her in tag lines. I drop the kids at school then duck into a nail salon where little fish nip away the dead skin hardening my heels. I'm in no rush for work. I crave touch. A mechanical fist kneads out the twists in my back.

A week later, it happens: A brush, a tap. At first I do nothing, believing it to be accidental, someone underestimating distance between moving things, poor spatial relations, lacking depth perception. But then I feel it again—on my shoulder, a meaningful squeeze. I look left, right. It's all a blur of runners.

Pssst. The sound cartoonish, as if uttered by a trench-coated PI. But when I check again I see him: the runner behind me, maybe 55, nose wide and flat, staring straight ahead. He shoots a thick coil of goo into his mouth, tosses the fuel packet into a bin on the curb.

He pulls out in front, and I follow. He ducks down a side path. This is my first deviation. We wind through the woods, up a hill, down a ravine, light winking through the branches, a canopy of century-old trees, and when we come out of the shadows into a clearing, the entire natural world is fucking.

It's like that Bosch triptych Adam and I saw on our Madrid honeymoon. Muscle tops and jumpsuits, marathon insignia stuck to wet T-shirts, compression sleeves shriveled in the grass like spent condoms. There are bodies and more bodies, men with men, women with women, men and women, a panorama of skin. The field pulses in a unified wave: low, rhythmic, ritualistic, adhering to a tacit under-standing. The lifelong runners are breaking in the new. I'm not even halfway into my routine, barely flushed, but as I bend to tighten my shoes I feel a hand in the damp of my shorts, cupped and calm. His scent is pickled cabbage. He steers me toward a tree. I have been married 15 years. For 15 years, Adam has said, Nothing is free. No stranger has so much as sprung for my latte let alone opened into me. I wrap my arms around the trunk. The pressure is not unwelcome, like a medical instrument. I tilt my hips. The sky is a piercing blue.

The sneaker salesman was right. Be patient, he'd said. Run through the pain and you will get past it, to the pleasure on the other side. Sure enough, here I am. I drink raw green juice, celery. I stop sneaking cigarettes out the window. I do squats, jacks, and flamingo stretches while flipping chicken breasts in a pan. I replay every detail from that morning: the caw of birds, stipple of clouds, errant plants torn wildly at the root.

My weekly mile count rises: 17, 22, 25.

"What's gotten into you?" Adam says.

"Inspiration." I kiss him, buoyant, light. I strap my phone band to my arm and take the porch two steps at a time. On the path my feet have begun to anticipate every dip and curve. Familiarity is a selling point to almost anything. People like to know what they're getting themselves into.

At the office, I search the Internet: How to run like a runner. I hold my shoulders at right angles and high-pump my knees in my chair. I breathe in through the nose, out through the mouth, to a count of four. I sound like a ventilator. A coworker peers over my cubicle. We are a real estate firm so everyone is up in each other's business. The videos say to run with big dick energy. How'd you get the exclusive on Maple, Trish? Barney says. You're not even full time. I shut my laptop, tell Barney to look between his legs. Then I blow off an open house appointment and head back to Paradise for a second run.

When I get home Adam asks: "How was your day? Any offers? Any bites?"

An associate broker circulates an email. It's about Dr. Ruth. The nonagenarian has issued a PSA: Runners make better lovers. Of course, people are paid to say anything, but it's eerie, the serendipity. Ruth's voice on the recording sounds like my grandmother, long dead, so now I'm crying into my hummus.

I consider forwarding the video to Adam, but sex is not where we are weak. Sex is where we are strong, our bodies so deeply cut by each other it takes next to nothing to generate heat. Without mouths or hands we come together and fit. Like Velcro. Like plugs to sockets, Lego pieces in a trademarked kit, we make each other whole. And hum. This is who we are.

The school year comes to a close. To celebrate, we say: how about some hot fudge sundaes? The kids say, how about screen time instead?

Mostly it is a summer like any other.

Mornings I am fucked in Runner's Paradise. I can't get enough. Old, young, flabby, tight, dreadlocked, androgynous; details are immaterial. I follow where I am led, maybe 50 spots in the woods, a lot of ground to cover. If the body wants what it wants, then each body is unknowable, caked in its paste, each lap around the park desirable and new. I cycle through the wiseass T-shirts, SUCKA and I PASSED

YOU, fuel belts unhinged, holsters for water and energy bars and caffeinated beans. I've never felt so alive.

Adam cops my thigh.

"I'll be a monkey's uncle," he says. The late show we've grown up on has taken a dip in ratings. The anchor looks wan. "Has the world lost its funny bone?" He clicks off the TV. I roll toward him. I am firmer all over, a plank of muscle, but he goes for my forehead instead.

"Your face—"

"What now?"

"It's glowing!"

I tell him I made a sale.

He hops downstairs in his gym shorts and cracks open champagne. The flutes are cloudy with dust.

"Don't get ahead of yourself. It's only a starter home."

He raises his glass: "To starts."

Then, just like that, it stops. I put on my fancy stretch top, my lucky pants. I lift my chin, square my shoulders, do my Kegel repeats; I point my elbows in. I run and wait and run and wait but nothing. What gives? I try to buck up, keep at it. Adam slaps aftershave on his jaw. The man never quits. My toenails blacken, fall off; I'm shedding pounds, my hair thins to wisps. I glide on lube where my nipples are bloody and chafed. I brush up against a newbie and he tells me to watch it, momma. He shouts, Stay in your lane.

I'm desperate to get back to Runner's Paradise. I turn off the main trail, turn onto dogs and owners, an oasis of man and beast. I hide behind a forsythia bush. Men are wearing leashes, neon orange slung at the hips. Dogs are running free. Dogs gather by the pond like office gossips around the water cooler. Dogs catch Frisbees with their teeth.

Where have I gone wrong? I veer off, off, off. Children scramble around their strollers for a picnic. Sunbathers lounge on towels. Hippies shake tambourines. Wheelchairs flaunt flags of every color. This one's deserted, a charred pit in the grass. Safety cones stacked like birthday hats on one side of the hole. The entire area is walled off in police tape, two, three times over, taut and strained, like ropes around a fight ring.

By fall, I have retraced every possible path. Whatever once was is gone. All that's left: dirt, ducks, scooters and kids. Uncle, I think. My feet are leaden, my throat scratched. The universe wins. I crawl to the couch, call in sick, stop leaving the house.

Adam comes home with a big shiny box wrapped in ribbon.

"Open it," my children say. Adam props me up and calls me his birthday girl. He draws the blinds. I say, Another year already, and he says, Thankfully. Either that or you're dead.

It is a ceramic bouquet of flowers.

"Don't they look real?" Kylie sticks the bow on my cheek.

"Realer than real." I blink into the autumn light.

Leaves change color: fire reds, toasted orange, brown curls like chocolate shavings. Wind rattles the windows. I place my hand to the glass and feel the whirl in my blood, prickles in my legs. Never in a thousand years would I have thought—but I don't think. I miss. The missing is an ache, a gnawing, a phantom limb. My sneakers are where I left them. I lace up. Cold whips my ears, veins crack like clay, but I am out the door. I am running again.

Toward the home stretch, I see him: my husband. I sneak up alongside him. Without looking, I can feel him follow, the swish of shorts, the shuffle of feet on loosely packed earth. Together we slink off the main path. Our bodies move in sync. We run past the make-shift sandbox, the memorial garden of rare plants, the kite flyers and peace-loving drummers, young girls braiding each other's hair. Without talking, Adam and I lie down on a bed of rotting leaves, hold each other deep in the woods.

NEIGHBORS

To your left, hipsters. Musicians to your right. Behind you, bankers and lawyers. At night, the dust of stars. A harvest moon brave as Jupiter sits on your roof as a reminder the whole world is not worth giving up. Which isn't to say a moon can fill you, but maybe it's a start. Go outside already. A spider you don't know by name does her work in the doorframe and you plow right into it, ruining her viscous string meant to keep you in or out. A car roars. Tricked out speakers, engine gunning, the works. Who isn't crying out for something? Around the corner, a car alarm's been at it for hours. In the morning there will be a sack of shit on the windshield, a gift from neighbors. It is impossible to know. Your street is long and shady. The waft of weed as common as dogs because neighbors need company. This one has a ball hoop. That one, a trampoline. Once upon a time, children played Kick the Can. Street hockey after school until the dads pulled in. One dad killed his wife in the bathtub while their toddler slept. News cameras parked on lawns reported the story: call girl debt + life insurance = freedom. The algorithm laid out on a piece of scrap paper. Google it. Not what you'd expect from suburbia but then nothing is. Another died in his armchair as the World Series played on

TV. The doctor two-doors-down made a house call but what can you do. Hearts stop. That doctor left his marriage for another woman or maybe a man. The chemist housed lab rats in his basement. From his cellar window you could hear the collective suck of water bottle teats, smell the exhaust of his fabric softener. Why are clouds of comfort so bad for the planet? It's hard not to think about dying. How would you do it? Brainstorm but you've lost your creativity. That's part of the problem. Your husband says it's not depression, it's being home all day every day. You need to get out, to see people. Your husband says he would want to kill himself too if he had your life. He means well and you know what he means. Take a walk. Go to the pharmacy, fill your prescription, stock up on children's vitamins. You buy the crappiest off-brand aluminum foil because you don't wish to outlive it. The glint of Freddie Krueger's hands once sent you running from sleepovers. Children tossed your lovey in the oven. This is your horror story. Violence is everywhere. The neighborhood has changed, no judgment, only of course there is. Why should anything stay the same? Check out the hair and shoes on the actor across the street who gets drunk on his porch and watches you. Some people are home. You've been home for years. Thank God for squirrels. One house was the color of an inner ear. Used to be a hotel, went the rumor. On Halloween, blood pumped through a dummy scaring the hell out of you but you've always been scared. Those neighbors had mice as pets, cats, too, and a Christmas tree 20 feet tall that stood in the hall shedding needles till spring. Lance Jezebel ran for public office and lost, Janice Proctor ran for school council and won. Both were haunted by scandal. Shari Johnson with juvenile diabetes invited you over to watch her pee on a stick. You played Weebles until they all fell down. Children on the trampoline jump higher, their voices lifting. A pair of ancient oaks frame a house of swingers. Renters keep their lights on, bone-thin curtains giving way to laughter, shadows, bodies. Can they hear you jerk it three stories up? Do they know how alone you are? In the house on the corner, where the sidewalk dropped off, you broke the picket fence. Everyone was young then. These days, holiday decorations go missing. People are suspicious. You no longer know who is Tina Turner, who is Frankenstein. Elvira runs marathons in your sleep. The garage door opens onto the initials of children who came before you, smashed pinky balls against brick spelling A-S-S. You know this game. Marvin Price's daughter got bigger but never grew up. She still plays dolls and Barry Manilow albums. In her mind, it is forever 1983. A new neighbor dies, cancer. No one comes to mourn. The Russians keep their children on a leash, a bachelor named Kelvin keeps to himself until his T-top breaks down on the Parkway and he is instantly crushed. Supposedly, your house once belonged to hoarders but you moved in empty. There's little a paint job and a savvy real estate agent can't handle. The walk is littered with ginkgo nuts, horse chestnut pods reminiscent of morning stars. Neighbors shack up on the top floor while scaffolding overruns their living room. They're not the only ones under construction. Your gutters are overflowing again. On trash days, you roll out the trash but the raccoons have been getting to it so you sit on the step with your strobe, with your frozen pizza suggestive of cheese, sit and wink that big yellow light, beam and shine in the dark and wait for eyes to flash back at you.

THE FEELING YOU WANT

My mom said if I was hell-bent on slime, it'd be on my own dime, so I saved up tooth and lunch money, then walked to the dollar store where nothing's a dollar to fill up on food coloring, shaving cream, Borax.

"That stuff will kill you," she said, so I went back and exchanged the rat poison for saline, which cost $11.99, leaving little for glue, the essential ingredient. I had to settle on generic but you should never settle, especially with slime.

I brought everything home and set up shop.

Mostly, my mom left me alone. Sometimes, I could hear her outside my door.

Once, she said, "Why not make something useful instead?"

By useful she meant brownies, a scarf. Crafts are her solace. My mom can knit two purl two until acorns drop free, provided there are no sleeves or seams.

"There's more to life," my dad said, then left to get it.

My ratios were off. I concocted a soupy bowl of glue, a pool of shaving cream. My fingers stuck together like a Popsicle raft.

My mom came in.

"It smells like your father's face."

I didn't look up. She went on breathing.

I said, "Do you mind?"

She sniffed. "A man's smell does not belong on a ten-year-old."

I told her I like it and she said, Wash your hands before dinner.

I was frustrated by my results yet determined.

America, my dad said. The land of infinite chances.

Food coloring didn't help. I texted my friend Lee, *Epic fail.* Lee wrote, *trust the recipes. No substitutes. Haven't you watched the videos?*

Ofc, I wrote. Nobody gets an idea off the top of their heads.

On YouTube, the girls have names like Brandy and Siena and Brianne. They have bedrooms with decals on the walls and mood paint and posters of other rising YouTube stars. Plush unicorns swing from plush moons. Comforters match rugs.

Lee was right about quality. We're only as good as the sum of our parts. Saturday, thanks to name brands, my slime cooperated. I finally got somewhere.

My mom told me to clean up my mess.

"Everything will dry out if you don't cap your crap."

"I forgot." I was distracted, too focused; I was not sorry.

"It's all such a waste."

I was not about to go there.

"What's the appeal?"

"Visual meditation," I said, tapping the screen. I worked the clump in my fist. The YouTube girls call it soul glue. "Just watching will improve your mood."

"There's nothing wrong with my mood," she said, but she leaned in.

On YouTube, the girls' hair shines like crazy diamonds (there are clips for that, too. Egg yolks, mayonnaise.) That's my dad's line. Instead of good night, he says, shine on, you crazy diamond. Once, I sang it to my brother, Jeb, before bed and my mom said, Don't sing that anti-Semite in my house.

"But we're not even Jewish."

"That's besides the point."

The point is, can you ever like the music without liking the man?

Sunday she ate herself into oblivion. Eating is better than drinking or whatever, but then she conked out on the couch, crumbs on her chest.

"Go easy on your mother," Dad said. "Put Mini-Me on."

That's his name for Jeb. If my dad is into himself, my mom is out of herself. It has nothing to do with size, Dad said, and everything to do with women, eating their feelings.

"Carbs are a zombie drug."

"I love zombies," Jeb said into the phone.

Jeb wet his pants at school. Accidents happen, but there was no extra set to change so Jeb had to borrow another kid's. Nothing fit right. Had it been me, I would've cried my face off, but people are better adjusted the second time around. No one showed at pick-up, so we sat at the pizza parlor across the street with our coats on, licking garlic knots, watching profiled suspects on the local news.

Later, my mom would say it was my dad's day and my dad would claim he sent Lucinda, why didn't we see her? Were we playing tricks? Lucinda works in his office and appreciates his shaved chest in a way that Mom never did.

While we waited, I took out a pale knob of homemade slime. It stretched like taffy, so Jeb tried to eat it.

"Don't eat it, dummy."

I showed him how to knead. Punched and poked and folded it over and pulled at the corners until the slime grew soft and warm. That's the hardest. In the videos, touch doesn't translate. You really have to stay with it to achieve the feeling you want. Jeb molded his wad into a ball, the kind you get for a quarter in the candy machine, and bounced it. The slime sprang back, embedded with hot pepper flakes and bits of straw wrapper.

"Stinks," he said.

"Don't I know it."

Today, my mom barges in. I've left crusty bowls and spoons on every surface like a junkie, like a cereal-addled college student, and she can't take it.

"Slime is taking over our lives."

I say, "That's not true. Besides, it's my business."

"Do you know there's a national glue shortage? Classrooms aren't getting what they need—"

"Sssssssssh. Pagana is demonstrating a new glow-in-the-dark recipe."

"Pagana, really?"

"Some parents are actually creative," I say. That shuts her. Whoever is shooting Pagana films a close-up of her hands—nails painted, neon, zigzag,

My mom sighs. "Can you at least try to contain it?"

"About that..."

I give her side-eye and she lets out a laugh and I jump, it's been so long since I've heard it, which makes her laugh more, so we sit like that on the edge of my bed, watching, my mom combing her nails through my hair.

To make up for things, Lucinda buys Jeb an Xbox game. All we need is an Xbox. Lucinda reddens. "I thought all kids had those."

For me, she gets an all-you-can slime kit. An obvious move, but my skills start to soar. Fluffy slime, marshmallow slime, glitter, butter slime, you name it. I name them Fairy Surprise, Lunar Lava. Lee dubs me *The Incredible Slime Master!*

We catch my mom narrating to herself as she clears the table. It starts as a mutter: This is how to cut grease from a pan. How to peel a carrot; slice an apple the night before school so it won't turn brown in the bag. When marriage becomes a mirror, smash the goddamn mirror. She breaks it down into steps, as if she has an audience. Step one, she gets louder. Wrings out her sponge. Step two. The disposal roars. My dad forbids me from having an online presence, which I guess is some sort of protection, although from what, I'm not sure. I don't know that he can protect me from anything.

In the morning, my mom drops to her hands and knees, pinches the rug.

"What's with the Styrofoam insanity?"

"Floam. The secret weapon. These puppies makes the slime slimier."

"Does the environment mean *anything* to you?"

I tell her the floam was a gift.

"Then keep it at your father's. You *do* do this there, right?"

When I don't answer she says, "Do you do anything at his place besides come home starving?"

Last time, Lucinda made cauliflower rice, which I kept to myself. If women eat their feelings, then what kind of feeling is that?

My mom looks at my hand like I'm offering her snot, so I press it into her palm and tell her to feel.

Lee pipes, "What do you think, Mrs. P? Does Jane have a future?"

My mom smells her fingers, Gypsy Stardust, then wipes on her jeans. "Don't get your hopes up."

"MOM," I say—*Can't she admit I'm good at something?*—but then she offers to film us if we agree to bake cookies with her.

"Start a channel. Call yourselves the sweet bots."

Lee grabs an apron. "Could I be any more jelly of your life?"

When I return from the weekend, my house smells different. My mom has been busy cleaning. Slime containers, caput. Bowls and spoons, no longer. No vials of dye. The whole operation erased. I lick my thumb and pick up a stray speck of foam.

I text Lee. *Ur not going to believe this [poop emoji].*

My mom calls me to the kitchen.

"How could you?" I scream.

She flings open the cupboards. There, behind closed doors, is my body of slime, organized by style and color, shelved in neat Tupperware towers like my own Sephora franchise. Jeb stands beside her on a step stool, poking his tongue in the hole where he lost his first tooth.

"Lids, love. Now, maybe they'll keep."

NO TIME FOR LOSERS

"What is it with you and these people?" My husband says. He is standing in the archway to the family room. The kids are asleep and I'm on the floor fenced in fresh laundry. After the weekend, it's back to folding. He nods at the TV. It's a cable program on the housebound obese. The show features people, real people, on their journey to weight loss: from doctors' visits and therapy couches, tearful fits and ultimatums to the final, begrudging agreement that they'll do it, if for no one else than for the kids (always for the kids) at which point experts descend upon the scene in khakis to sweep up tubs of fried chicken, bags of chips, and jumbo cups as the terrified, wide-eyed subjects brace themselves against metal strongholds, ladders filched slick from the deep end, and slowly, huff by labored puff, stand up.

"It's inspiring," I say. "Look how they turn their lives around."

"It's sick," Steve says. "A goddamn circus."

I shake out a shirt. Whenever I do housework I dose up on reality: *Hoarders*, pregnant teens, interventions. Watching other people is a distraction. It takes me out of myself. I tuck one sleeve, then another. The pile rises. I press and smooth.

Steve calls them *garbage humans.*

He says, "Have they no shame?"

And yet, Steve believes in free trade. Sell anything: Organs, options, same diff. I ball socks, arrange them into a pyramid. He runs the edge of a business card between his long front teeth.

We'd gone upstate with Steve's college buddies. An Independence Day tradition: to rent out an arts and crafts cabin on the Delaware with a bright expanse of windows facing the river, prize stag's heads on display, tapestries of the American flag. To eat like pigs, play cards and Frisbee golf, to get wasted and act out charades. Over the years the rentals have been upgraded, as have the wives, periodically it rains, our hair is no longer what it was; otherwise the weekends are interchangeable, equally pleasant and dull.

The vacation started out fine. When it comes to Steve, there are a few rules. Follow them and you're in business. My husband likes routine, results. Tangibility. Discover what works and stick with it. To psych himself up for the trip, he jumped rope, wiggled chin-ups on the bar. He made playlists and custom T-shirts, unearthed his college dugout and bat and packed it tight with sativa in the front seat. On the drive, we smoked one-hitters, his arm out the window, my scalp burning with the top down until he spotted me a baseball cap. It smelled like his scalp. We said things like "Pass the peace pipe." We punctuated with "hon," the way you do with intimates or strangers. Life was easy. We were in, in, in.

We were the first to arrive. If nothing else, Steve has a heavy foot and an unflagging sense of direction. A carved eagle and whittled Sioux greeted us, the kind sold at outposts by the side of a country road. I unpacked the car. Steve went on a beer run. We chose the largest room, wood paneling, private bath with a plastic coated tub like the one I gave birth in. This was the extent of our advantage. Next came Kelly and Chris with matching luggage and snapshots of their latest renovation, followed by Smitty and his young wife, Daphne; Rodger with Sue's lifted boobs. Harlan and LeAnn pulled in last, after completing their sixth triathlon with personal bests. Muscles bulged through their clothes, which fit like superhero skins.

Competition is human nature. I understand. I watch *Survivor.* I watch *The Bachelor.* I follow cameras wherever they go. It's normal to want to keep score. Striving is the engine of desire. Life is not a dress rehearsal, say the network hosts. No time for losers: these were his bros, his Sigma Chai brothers. Still, maybe I should have tried harder to puff him up to scale. That first night while we sat around the porch with drinks and fancy pickles, I could have been more sympathetic as the sun set and Steve's face fell like a sad pup listening to the litany of everyone else's achievements. I could have squeezed his hand, trailed my fingers along the slope of his neck as it blotched red with envy. I could have strummed the lobe of his ear and said: You are plenty. You are more than enough.

But I'm his wife.

Immediately, Steve started in. Nearly knocked over his chair when he sprang up, pacing like a *Shark Tank* contestant. His big idea: to place bets. Who could out-shit, out-cook, out-fish, out-canoe, who could drink the others into oblivion. The man needs an audience. Otherwise, he is a tree falling in the woods. Even our five-year-old throws fart contests with playmates, which is to say—you're never too young to join the rat race. A beer bong and egg timer materialized, for kicks. The guys called him genius. The wives chuckled along because we didn't want to feel left out, like we were missing something, depth or experience or wedge of common ground. We refilled glasses. Sue pulled a vaporizer from her purse, iridescent blue, the word INHALE stamped on the side, the name of her yoga studio. It kept our hands busy. The night was beautiful, warm yet crisp, the bats flapping from tree to tree. Bourbon bombs, Moscow mules. The hot tub bubbled away on the patio.

Within hours, bets turned to sex. Steve devised a code word to keep things polite. The code word was checkers. Under the super moon the men high-fived. Steve lit the grill, the pinnacle of his culinary prowess: steaks, lobsters, octopi in their entirety, face down and prostrate, tentacles charred and all.

"An octopus has three hearts." I learned it from our kid's *Weird But True* book.

"A lobster mates for life," Daphne chimed in.

Like I said, she was new.

"Let the games begin," Steve said, trailing me into the bathroom. I turned on the faucet. He came around from behind, his arms in Heimlich position. The room had mirrors on all walls, like a discount department store's dressing room. I shut the tap, dried my hands and backed into him. I'd made a life out of backing into things.

"King me," he pounced an hour later. I smiled wide enough to break my face. My teeth red with wine. No one noticed. They were playing, too. It was a holiday weekend, our great nation's birthday. Let freedom ring! Harlan and LeAnn stormed the open-area loft, gymnastic on bunk beds. Daphne and Smitty took the Jacuzzi. We padded around in clammy bathing suits. My navy one-piece had a ruffle that draped like a bib, making me feel both infantile and ancient.

"Does it turn you on?" Steve says now of the show. This is not dirty talk. I have not been punished adequately. I am sorry but not sorry enough, not sorry for what he wants me to be sorry for. When did his desires ever warrant apology?

He says, "It's amazing how they live with themselves."

How does anyone? I want to say, but stop myself. We live in a split-level with stapled carpet on the commuter line in the wrong school district. Our TV is a relic by today's standards.

I fold a negligee—once pink, now gray. Lace unravels. It's from our honeymoon. Steve loosens his tie. I get it. He works. I breast-feed. I play Candyland while life leaks from me, but at the end of a day, he's beat. The show goes to commercial. Underwear models in wings announce a runway special. They leg the stage in satin and pink. Steve hooks his finger in his knot, leans against the molding. An ad pops on for bleach.

Before all of this, who was I? Honestly, it's hard to remember. My parents died in rapid succession—one by accident, one by despair—killing the so-called formative years. That's grief. Only so much room in the prefrontal cortex, I heard on talk radio. Pixar made a movie about it, which I dragged my kids to even though they're too young to understand, but sometimes you need to get out and eat popcorn and cry in a dark theater with strangers. The brain purges nonessentials, such as, but not limited to, feelings, moments, other loves.

Checkers. Here was a game we all could rally behind. The spirit was contagious. It made joiners out of us. Saturday, the cabin began to smell from our fervor. We cranked ceiling fans, fried eggs and bacon over the chlorinated funk, then opened the windows and rushed to the river. Downstream, the color of birch beer, I shivered. Boulders jutted like headstones and I held on, careful not to be carried by the current. When clouds rolled in we pulled ourselves onto the river-bank. Guys stood around dripping. Wives served lunch: cold cuts beneath wire nets designed to keep out insects. Toothpicks turned into mini-duels, snapped into useless weapons.

Steve said, "Pass the mustard, hon."

I passed.

"You're the best," he squeezed my thigh.

Who doesn't appreciate attention? We'd arrived at the age of irrelevance, the lot of us—except for Daphne, who was not yet 30—so any acknowledgment fed our hunger. Earlier in the week, Steve grumbled he'd been kept off email chains at work until he realized that email chains themselves were a thing of the past. I felt bad. The world was moving. Our idols, dying. There was not a hip hairdo in sight. I made a bologna sandwich, sawed it in two.

Tonight's episode is dedicated to enablers, a Valentine's special. It is a re-run but not to me. On screen lovers fatten and feed. "More to love," partners say of their 800-pound spouses, boyfriends and girlfriends. They curl into the warm contours of their bodies. They relish plenitude. But the wellness experts aren't having it. They barge into basements snapping clipboards. Hut, hut. Break it up. They mistake love for abuse. Pull apart couples melded like two halves of grilled cheese with clear instructions to stop the fetishizing madness. It's like a crackdown from *Cops* only the enemy is devotion. The world's leading health professionals issue a warning: Morbidly is more than obese's descriptor. Death is imminent. People need to know empty in order to know full. "No wonder you feel the way you do," Steve says, although I haven't said anything. Do misers of the heart have a better chance at survival? He's opened his collar, revealing a lean crescent of undershirt, a patch of chest hair. "Dogs, left to their own devices, will eat themselves to death, too." He says this as absolution, as if to say, everyone struggles with impulse control. This is Steve softening, conceding. He is coming around. Eventually, Steve will retreat, like a pet whose pleas for affection have gone unanswered.

I move on to the kids' clothes: tiny undershirts with block prints and snaps in the crotch. On screen, determination takes root. Welcome to reality. Thighs weep in high definition. Pleats of flesh bow to knees.

It's not entirely passive. Steve has this way of walking like he's stomping on grapes, like he's rolling up his pants and really going for it. We honeymooned in Napa. The landscape arid and green, but I stayed in bed beneath a pouf of white eyelet trying to stitch my choices together. Here I was. Not that it was bad. Steve was not a bad person. Steve took care of my wine headaches. I liked the idea of being taken care of. When it didn't end up as I imagined, I stopped imagining.

Steve thunders around our house like he needs to be heard. Pop of the fridge, slide of the crisper—Steve searching for something fresh and well-balanced—but he will not find what he's looking for. I haven't bought what he wants.

Last weekend, in the heat of checkers, we kept track on a chalkboard, fingers dusted in pastel. Slashes crossed, multiplied by the bundle. Our numbers rose. My ambition grew.

At first, Steve was into it. He dealt me a squeeze, called me a "go-getter."

But the thrill soured quickly. My advances were smothering him. The dynamics were off. Why must I shove him out of the driver's seat?

"Okay, let's give it a rest."

Only I was just getting started. I'm not sure what came over me. Victory, I could taste it, my lips tingling like I'd overdone the hot sauce. I could be a champion.

Steve wanted to return to the guys. *The guys!* That's why we were here. Before checkers, after checkers, the guys drank beers. Balanced canoes on their heads like water jugs. They cliff jumped. I felt stricken. People break their backs on rusty stoves sunk at the bottom of rivers. My mother had drowned. I'd watched her clear as July from the jagged slip of Watkins Glen. Come back! I urged. Men became boys in mid-air, sized up their splashes. They sat phone-to-phone enlisting in adventure races, Steve paling as he calculated his chances and adjusted for loss, assuring himself it was always better to be one of the guys than to back down.

I was not backing down either. "Pussies!" I shouted.

"Hon," Steve said. "What's eating you?"

I can't say I planned it. But I couldn't sit around with the other wives talking about what was for dinner. I was tired of nice. I grabbed Steve by the wrist.

This time, the guys were on my side.

"Dude. Bro. What are you waiting for?"

In the bedroom, I arranged a makeshift tripod, propping my phone against a whittled duck. I pressed record.

"Kills the mood," Steve said, inching down. I'll give him this: The man gets a job done. Only that day, I felt nothing. Not even numb. The red light blinked. I shut my eyes. There had to be another way. Cinch my wrists; clamp my throat, I wanted to be berated.

"Say it!"

Steve popped up. "Say what?"

"I am your garbage human!"

With that, the duck decoy fell over. The guys poked their faces in the door.

"You try to satisfy her." Steve stormed out.

They came in.

Later, we watched the clips—Chris dropping his towel, the gathered slick of Smitty's back. Harlan, with his armored jaw, yanking my hair and twisting. In the shower, we slipped and slid. Soap filled my eyes. I teared up. I knew these guys. We'd all gone to college. My body is no longer young but it is a body that has served me, as much as a body can, as a repository for memory. It is a body whose want knows no limit. Images jumped and skittered but there was a discernible look on my face, a curl in my lip. Neither pleasure nor despair. Nor was it resignation. A taut line, halfway between. Like the goddamn Mona Lisa. Here I was: winning. I almost won. No one mentioned monogamy. Still, when Daphne caught wind of it, bless her pure heart, I was disqualified. The whole game thrown out.

Steve and I drove home in silence.

Plot twist: without food, love loses expression. Relationships suffer. The couple on TV mourns for what they once had. Failure to adapt— our planet's biggest downfall. In a role reversal, the husband tries to stuff himself instead of his wife. He vomits mango-colored chunks. The wife wails from her bed that she is starving. She is still the same size but now there's an enormous hole inside her. In the next clip, the wheelchair disappears. The housebound wife learns to walk again. Cue the music: The husband throws a party with mylar balloons.

Do I feel bad? Of course I do. I mean, all the time.

My sister Kate says that's normal. We are only what we allow ourselves to become. She is younger but wiser. Her relationships live and die via text. I wear yoga pants though I've never done yoga.

Steve says, "Haven't you seen enough?"

He is back with his snack. I hear food sounds, breathing. I mute the TV. The show marches on silently. It can't be easy, being Steve. He provides and I don't even put away dishes. We're just going to reuse them, but Steve says, If only you took more pride in the little things.

One thing I remember: Steve and I on the couch those early days. Maybe we were high or maybe we were just into each other, but either way we were sitting there, laughing and talking and snacking. He held up a cracker.

"You can tell a lot about a person by how they eat."

"That so?" I grabbed the box.

"Some take everything at once, like communion."

He shot a cracker through his lips. I nibbled at the edges of mine in termitic fury, flaking bits on my jeans, until the buttery round disappeared.

There's no happy ending. Health problems don't evaporate with weight loss. Flaps of skin, wide and winged as stingrays, present a new burden.

FUPA, the plastic surgeon calls it. His nose pointy, sharp as a pin. The camera zooms on his teeth as he translates the acronym, suppressing a laugh. The surgeon is accustomed to Beverly Hills housewives, a recurring guest on multiple reality shows.

He clicks his pen. "When was the last time you saw yourself pee?"

The wife's body no longer fills its casing, but the surgeon says this is good news: "FUPA can be tailored and shaped, trimmed off like grist on a good steak. "

Lovers weep in paper gowns. Afterward, the camera cuts to the operating table, a marbled heap. It looks like custard. I think about what it must be like to let go of weight, without disastrous side effects like flesh eating bacteria, necrosis. The show wraps on a cliffhanger, the future, unknown. The postscript rolls: after multiple procedures, the couple has split. Their new bodies have found new selves to love.

I shut the TV.

"Thank you," Steve says. His speech is garbled, as if he's rolling a mouthful of dice. Grapes I'd thrown in the freezer. I listen to him suck thickly then chew.

RABBI TALES

I tell my therapist I'm in love with my rabbi. Like the start of a joke, only no joke. I haven't even seen that show about the hot priest. Apparently, my therapist says, it's more common than you'd think.

I'm not sure what it is. I'm not a spiritual person. Although I wouldn't actively *deny* an insider scoop, an on-ramp to nirvana, typically such quests amount to smoking weed alone in my apartment. Shortcuts have never panned out.

Nevertheless, here I am in this house of worship.

Why does anyone wander into shul on Yom Kippur? Superstition, boredom, loneliness. Check all boxes that apply. An urge to atone— *for what?* My years have contained no large drama. But, then, it's always the little things.

My mother froths with joy. Way to get out and meet people! In my day, she says, but it's no longer her day. Today is all swipe left right from the hull of the couch.

Most of the men here are widowers. Husbands, too, with shiny shoes and shiny wives and children with shiny chins. They sit in the back with me. The front row is arthritic. No kidding about changing times, Mom. A house of prayer is no longer the center of Jewish life. What's left is the temple of death.

Last time I showed up, ladies from the sisterhood tried to rope me into their weekly challah bake, their can collection, but I keep nonperishables to myself. I blew off their book club, though I did throw a little elbow grease into packaging their Emergency Go Kits. Today they congregate in the bathroom—marathon day of prayer, and the annual appeal feels grubby even to the givers. They roll stubby lipsticks, smack blot kiss, address each other in the mirror. What did you think of the rabbi?

This is what we do. Rate the clergy. We judge in our Keds. I didn't care for his spiel last week, one lady says. Too political. Not political enough. Couldn't hear a thing.

No one can make everyone happy all the time, I say and they frown, which makes me love my rabbi even more.

I return to my nosebleed seat with the other once-a-year faithful. My rabbi is at the pulpit in his caftan, kittel—his ceremonial, nearly diaphanous shroud—what the holy wear on holy days, to experience an intimacy unencumbered by clothes, to leave their corporal selves behind.

Oh but his body, his face. Even from a distance, I feel a devout twinge, the Eternal Light glowing down on his scalp like a magic crystal. My legs buckle. Another non-member thrusts me the smelling salts circulating on fast days, cloves jammed into a lemon. It looks like a hand grenade. I inhale, deep.

"We ask ourselves: what matters? Why do we fear our fears?"

I'm touched, all the way in the back. He touches me. My rabbi makes me cry. It doesn't take much. His purity against my sin. Tonight, after the shofar signals the end or beginning, depending on your outlook, when we've all been inscribed and had a heel of bread, he'll offer a hug as I crumble. More like a pat. If you want to talk, you know where to find me. In my mind I'm carrying his dirty plate to the sink, our bodies bridged and woven like Chagall, like we've been bound together for ages.

I glance around, flushed—can everyone perceive our obvious heat?—but people are putting on coats, corralling children, rushing off to their own break fast invites for kugel, for bagels and lox. The room empties out.

After the holidays, I start going on Saturdays. Day of rest, but I'm vigilant. I feel his presence behind me. Like in high school, when Scott Hill crossed the cafeteria with his hot gravy tray. Slim crowd, so I move up. It's like watching a movie too large and too close. I save my rabbi a seat, even though he's on stage. I imagine him beside me in the pew, slipping off shoes, rubbing his toes along my eczematous arches. There is always a sponsored kiddush, the synagogue big on buffets, butter cookies embedded with sprinkles. I make him a plate, refill his cup.

He says, Good Shabbos. Nice to see you. How was your week?

One time he says, Are you much of a reader?

Yes, I pipe up. I read *and* I write.

Good, he nods. Remind me. There's this story, tell me what you think.

He's married, of course. A single rabbi makes the congregation nervous, like here's someone who can't commit, can't get anyone to trust him, to stay through thick and thin, to love him forever. That's never been my issue.

I tell my therapist. My therapist is my mother. Have you met someone? She asks. As a matter of fact, I say. Thank God. She fans herself, farklempt. I knew you'd find love. Love, I echo, though it sounds more like a question. Don't go jinxing it, she snaps. Say no more.

At night, he's in my dreams. Down dirt roads, possessed of blind faith and well-tread shoes. We're on the lookout for bears, skunks, raccoons as we run around the curves of the earth, step from the shadows into bright prairie light.

Where did you meet him? My mother, again.

Shul, I say.

She claps. What I tell you?

I add Friday to my Saturday routine. He doesn't always show. Sometimes it's the assistant rabbi. My rabbi has obligations, invitations. A macher like him is in high demand. A new mikvah needs his blessing. My rabbi and his wife now offer ritual bath services in addition to weddings, funerals. Like a spa minus the shvitz, the sisterhood tells me. The only thing lacking is a Russian masseuse. One sister shovels leftover babka into her purse. She'll freeze it and thaw it for shiva calls, when sitting for the dead. Why waste what's perfectly good?

Try it, my rabbi winks. Make a reservation. See for yourself.

I mark my calendar for my next bleed but I've become erratic. My eggs have begun to break off and thin, not that I want children. Children are one loss I'm not mourning but still, standing barefoot in the locker room, swabbing beneath my nails, it's hard not to feel that my body has become a withered apricot-like thing, without the reminder of touch.

The bath is so warm I have to pee. With his wife as witness, down I go, three times, a blessing, and she shields me with a towel, for my sake or hers, from my immodest ache.

Summer, he wears a yarmulke the size of the sun. The sky unfolds without a hint of humidity so we sit on the grass, knees folded like gurus—like the rabbi he is. My rabbi says a prayer over his Ziploc of psilocybin before we eat them, caps and stems, chewing slowly in deference to nature, to all living things. Who doesn't seek higher ground? Curiosity, magic mushrooms, an endless journey, amen. Without touching, we lie on our backs, an innocent dream, however real it feels, my hair spilling out, the ground tilting beneath us as it spins. Color trails begin. I say vessel, he says shatter. I say Isaiah, and he says something something God, something hope in the palm of your hand, prying mine open to trace my creases into the future. Maybe it's all manufactured, but that doesn't mean we can't play along, take whatever we can.

As for sex—the divine promise of transcendence—are they not one and the same? I wonder how my rabbi, all rabbis, navigate the power they lord over their base. All around are ugly stories.

To test my loyalty, I flit from shul to shul. They all smell of animal hide and breath. The rabbis drill into me like a third eye. They are fit enough, despite the hours mulling over brittle tomes in dim quarters, forgetting to eat, veiny in the wrists from a lifelong wrestle with doubt, of shouldering and dancing with the five books of Moses.

In Trader Joe's, he wears a concert T-shirt, his biceps popping out of the sleeves. I drop my peach. He picks it up, brushes it off.

Get you a fresh?

I tell him I'll keep the bruised.

My mother is furious. She's shopping with me, she's always with me, tracking my transgressions and impossibilities. Take the good. Is this your idea of love? If you can't live it, write it, my therapist suggests. Don't try so hard, just let yourself go.

Only you're limited in imagination. Your rabbi is of rabbinic age. Tall, not stooped, older but not too old, absent of hearing aids, young enough to stand up, sit down, hoist the chair for horas. He wears glasses because presbyopia strikes everyone, no matter how holy. Your rabbi tunnels through you with the elegiac tone of his *Unetanah*

Tokef and lowers to his knees for *Aleinu*, occupying the sweet spot on the generational divide as he sets his gaze on you, in the front, in the back, fiddling with the frayed silk bookmark of your siddur somewhere in the middle distance.

You have created him, so here he is.

In the rain. With a sack of cherries. On the path to redemption in Lycra and bicycle shoes. Reciting liturgy like lyric poetry in a field of Queen Anne's lace, strumming his guitar for freedom. You inch behind your rabbi for a back rub. He presses himself into your grip. Together you traverse gravel and pith, until you say, Where have you been all my life? And he says (because you get what you deserve): What life?

So you share an ice cream. Actually, he orders a cone. You slurp a milkshake so fast your head freezes, but then like everything, it passes as the sun slips behind the lake at the edge of town, turning you into children again.

BOUGIE NIGHTS

Larry Fischer had a new bitters kit he wanted to try, the kind packaged with letterpress and pipette. It accompanied his Cocktail of the Month membership, which we'd sprung for on his fiftieth birthday. Rich and I were beat, another bad night, but we couldn't pass on the invitation. The Kaplans were coming, as were Bonnie and Stu. Soon our kids would be leaving for college, and then what? Larry wheeled out his bar cart, petri dish of garnishes, fussy peels legging the rims of his lowballs like showgirls. He mixed. Yacht rock smoothed through in-wall speakers. The drinks were kicky and creative. *Bearded Lady, Boomerang, Dying Bastard*. We had a few, then a few more. No one was counting. It was Saturday night.

The trick is not to let a little thing become something bigger. Recent tax hikes, going-out-of-business sales. There's only so much to say to people before it's pulling teeth. The air felt stale. It was too cold to keep the windows open, too hot to keep them closed. Half-eaten phyllo triangles lay abandoned on chairs and nesting tables, napkins crushed like winter tulips. Someone suggested Pictionary, one of those stylish German board games, but that would require real concentration. A photo-realist painting of the Fischer family presided on the wall above the fireplace. Rich stared at it; my eyes watered. We were infected by yawns.

Gayle said, "What's with you? Your face is halfway down your face."

Leave it to Gayle. Our sons had gone to nursery together. I swirled my drink.

"Allergies," I said, crossing and uncrossing my legs. It wasn't like me to wear pantyhose. Gayle cocked her head in concern. The right thing would have been to get off the couch and help her plate dessert.

Gayle returned with a tray of petit fours. "Coffee, tea, me?"

We lived for easy laughs.

"Our circadian rhythms are shot," I said, popping a cake. I thought I sounded normal, but apparently, this was not my indoor voice. Wax builds over time. My hands looked gray. "Rich can't sleep. I can't stop sleeping."

"Trouble in paradise?" Bonnie cut in. Stu sprang alive. They wore matching socks and wrung out each other's knees. The group treated other people's misery like blood in shark waters. Shelley perked up from beneath Jeff's arm, more chokehold than embrace. When we first moved in, the Kaplans invited us over for their annual White Night, which culminated in Shelley diving naked into the pool. It was shaped like a magic bean and glowed like a higher planet from the underwater lights and everyone followed, shedding layers. Now, we recycled past themes. Larry had a cannabis cave and Atari in the basement but even nostalgia gets old. No one was venturing downstairs with a bag of Cheetos. It was not that kind of night.

Rich looked at me, haggard, tense in the jaw, like he used to get after a night out in the city. "Is this the time or the place?" Which was sweet, if you think about it, him trying to defend us, clinging to the quaint notion of privacy.

Bonnie clasped her palms together. She was wearing a tight purple turtleneck, which made her look like a bottle of salad dressing. "I had that with my first husband, Lou. New job, new pressures, and before you know it—"

Shelley said, "Don't overthink it. Thinking is the kiss of death." She wore rings, big dark gems that looked like eight-balls. "Maybe it's the moon, Joyce."

"One online workshop and she knows everything," Jeff said. He'd dropped considerable weight since his brother's heart attack. "Just get a king bed."

"Then you'll never touch each other again." Shelley pouted, needle-like grooves in her lips. There was a time we all were smokers.

Gayle smiled a smile that said, Smile. She'd had a double mastectomy at 39 and understood the power of positive thinking, Larry swung through the kitchen wearing an apron that said Bareback Your Barback, sleeves rolled, a towel on the shoulder. Larry always looked the part. He raised his eyebrows, shoved both hands in his armpits as if trying to warm them.

"Who died?"

We laughed. Rich stood. Palmed my head, said it was getting late.

In the morning, Rich looked like hell, his hair all grizzled and spiky. I had the spins and a metallic taste in my mouth but otherwise felt how I always feel. We drank balance smoothies with bright flecks of ginger and downloaded apps for meditation. We sat on mats as digitized voices spoke of enlightenment, we fanned our fingers in front of each other without touching, bowed heads, we drew breath when our phones said to breathe.

Why now, were we so out of whack? Why anything? We'd never been allergic before. Friends cited vitamin D deficiency, Monsanto. Something in the water. We read the newspaper. Others had it far worse. I could sleep through it. I could brush it under the rug and call it housekeeping.

Rich punched the pillow. I brought him a glass of warm milk.

"I'm not an infant," he said.

"Baby," I cooed. Insomnia takes work. "You can't just snap your fingers," I said. I splashed Bailey's in his cup and held it to his lips. I dug my pregnancy pillow out from storage. Some of the stuffing had started to poke through, dingy duck feathers, the case yellowed, thin. I don't know why I'd kept it. The shape was long and curved like a body. Fifteen years ago he called it my bitch. Now Rich hugged that bitch for dear life.

Of course, no one starts out like this. We'd been that couple on an ocean promenade, two plated halves of a gold charm that opened and shut on a latch. We'd fed each other grapes in the rain and zip lined through a jungle, just the two of us. Snapped our kids into travel packs and hiked the Grand Canyon. Flew to Florida, to the San Diego Zoo.

When Gayle got sick, we pitched in without question. Rich was the one who said there is more to a wife than meals. People have needs. The whole thing was his idea. Everyone agreed it was charitable. Gayle took my charity in stride. Larry was forever grateful. Sometimes Rich would watch in the dark while Larry flipped me over. It was easier for all of us without my face.

"Promise me," Rich said, in the bathroom, hectic with masks and powders and firming creams. He wants me to get rid of this gunk and clutter, but no one puts age-defying demands on him. I dipped into my mascara. Reflex: my jaw goes slack when I do my eyes. Today they kept tearing so the makeup wouldn't go on. He tossed his towel in the hamper. Eventually, I gave up.

"I promise," I said.

Gayle rang but I didn't have the energy. My chest hurt. The more I slept the more sleep I craved. I got in my car. She called again.

I said, "Have you ever felt like this?" I was soaked, hot flashes raging, as I backed out of the driveway. I drove past her house. Larry told Rich she'd relapsed. The curtains were closed.

"We've tried everything," I gabbed. In the produce aisle I saw Shelley sniffing the tush of a melon and waved, indicating the phone on my ear.

Gayle said, "Intimacy might help."

I said, "You'd think."

Oh but I dreamed. REM patterns stretched longer and deeper. Some mornings I couldn't get up. Why bother? In dreams, I spoke in an alluring British accent, solved high-profile crime in killer heels. I floated down the Seine in orange silk with a picnic basket on my wrist because lost in la-la land my body was like that—buoyant and lovely and young.

"What have you done with my wife?" Rich said when he came in tonight. I tried to laugh but my face barely moved. Bonnie had rec-ommended this new beauty tape to patch frown lines. Placebo can be its own cure. If you can't look like a mummy, like a victim of trauma in your own bedroom, then where can you be yourself?

"You're a nightmare," he said.

"Sleep tight," I said, shutting the light.

Like a good woman, I went to Bed, Bath, etc. for new shams and a mattress topper, bedding of Egyptian cotton. I bought Gayle a blender. Doused Rich's side with lavender oil, hung fragrant satchels off the bedposts like drying links of meat. One night I even sang lullabies a cappella until my voice cracked, as I'd done for the kids, but Rich flapped his book at me. "Stop, just stop it. Please."

He gritted his teeth. I suggested a bite plate.

"Larry will fit you one in his office for free." I mentioned meds, over-the-counter and prescriptions, but Rich said, "Pills can't cure everything."

A part of me loved his idealism.

The other part wanted to say, *Almost everything.*

"I don't know what my problem is," I told Shelley. I told Bonnie, even Gayle. We were always on the phone. "Sleep all day and I can still sleep at night."

"Your problem is—" Rich walked into the kitchen. He was back on coffee. He said something else, but I couldn't hear right. He didn't mean it. When people are that tired and grumpy they say all sorts of things.

As for the kids: they hardly spoke to me anymore. Allowance, keys to the car. What else is there? The kids walked through the house, dropped their bags, loaded up on snacks, then retreated to their rooms in combat boots. I could hear their keyboards clicking away as I paused in front of their closed doors, as I called out: *Good night, nobody. Good night, mush.*

The sound of sawing woke me. I'm not sure what time it was. *He-haw,* the whole bed shimmied and shook. I sat up. Rich's forehead glistened as he muscled the rough blade of his handsaw back and forth along the seams of the bed frame.

"Couldn't you wait?" I rubbed my eyes.

"I've had it," he said. His tongue darted around while he worked. Finally, he was being proactive, I had to give him that. His legs cramped, he was simply too big. In fact, he was shorter than me, but I stayed quiet, until the wood panels dropped to the floor and debris flew up in a cloud.

I looked down at our mess.

When the kids were small, Rich rescued a pregnant mouse from the lab and brought her home as a pet. Momma gave birth in a glass cage then proceeded to eat the two runts of her litter, dark as snails. The sawdust reminded me of that mouse bedding. Rich vacuumed it up, using the nozzle attachment in hard-to-reach corners until the whole room was clean.

Afterward, Rich conked right out, but my night was over. I thrashed from side to side. I coughed a lung, a gravelly wheeze. My nose dripped. I sucked a splinter. Gayle's reconstruction surgery had used leftover baby weight for breast tissue, granting her a bonus tummy tuck. Two-for-one special. Lucky her. Larry hadn't come by in months. At dawn, I got up. The bed sank to one side. Rich let out a snore. I would never sleep again.

"Better?" I said. "Happy now?"

AROMATHERAPY

That winter, we went to the desert for a girls' getaway. We were hardly girls. One of us was dying, Meredith had died; all of us had lost someone. It was a silent retreat. What was there to say? We were newly divorced and perennially single, we were stuck in marriages and dating online and pregnant with a—surprise!—third kid. For days we feasted on goji berries and posed as trees and paid gobs of money for strangers to touch us. For every ailment there was an oil. Remember the time we cut school and hitched down the shore for what's his name? Nobody said. Our skin cracked in the sauna and shriveled in group baths, but before leaving, we swaddled ourselves like babies in robes and sampled high-end products to take home, greasing our hands in jasmine and lavender and sandalwood, holding out fingers for each other to smell.

DON'T YOU SWIM?

If she's smart about it, Laura can survive the whole boat ride without incident. The boat, a 60-foot catamaran, accommodates 12 other families. Plus crew. Maybe it's not even him, standing at the port with his wife, her straw tote and rash-guarded twins. His Dartmouth cap is a giveaway, but maybe he won't recognize her. Abortion Roy. She will hustle to the stern and slather sunscreen on her children, pump and rub, hold on, lobster ears, the neck is always neglected, let me get in that crease and blend, she will fiddle with snacks and size out snorkeling masks while silently Jedi-ing his family to the prow. Even if their eyes meet, she can pull this off. College had taught her, among other things (semiotics, Saussure, the bus route to Planned Parenthood) how to master the I-Don't-See-You Game: a way of seeming engaged but aloof, gazing past a shoulder as if wrestling a problem of the universe too grave for the mere mortal in her field of view. She angles her chin to the sky. A pelican nose dives into the sea. She calculates. The trip would be an hour out, drop anchor, flutter with angelfish, then another 15. Once they reach the island, she will be free.

"Welcome, watch your step," the skipper says. He holds out his hand to women, but to women and children only, and she takes it, allowing him to ease her up the ramp. Laura acts according to plan, muscling to the back to secure seats with their stuff, spreading shovels and towels. The deck fills ups quickly. Once the captain finishes safety precautions, her husband rises to roam. It is a party boat and beer in hand, Evan wants to party. Who doesn't want to party? Family style, of course, he says, rustling the humid heads of the kids. Theo and Racine are five and nine. Theo wears floaties like blood pressure cuffs. Racine hocks fresh spit in her goggles, squeaks it around the lenses with her thumb. It is 9:30 in the morning. The wind kicks up; the water a choppy blue green, as if a satellite view of Earth had been fed through a blender. Laura's stomach churns. Abortion Roy. What were the chances? But then, this was the Caribbean in February, so here they were with half of suburban New Jersey. It was statistics, not fate. Laura knuckles the rail. Her hair whips her face.

"Boat drink?" Evan says.

"Sea sick." He tips his beer, nods, offers to drum up a Dramamine.

Within minutes, the men have found each other, ball caps covering bald heads in the signpost of fraternity. It's like a scene from Animal Planet: the glance and sniff, chests swelled to bumping. Already they are close talking. Laura's husband never misses an opportunity. You were in Hanover? My wife went to Hanover. Evan says Hanover instead of Dartmouth, like Harvard coeds claim Cambridge. Maybe you know each other. Laura! Evan waves, boisterous. He is proud of her pedigree. When he smiles, his dimple flashes and he looks like a boy—not Theo, plagued with her resting bitch face—but more like Racine, jaw thrust and ready to slurp up the world on a chilled half-shell. Evan is always telling Laura to put herself out there, be friendly, mingle, you never know who you might meet or what they might bring to the table. *It's never too late to start something.* His outlook would be a refreshing mist should ever she wish to be misted.

Now, as he tilts his bottleneck, her children clamber over her with their wants, chewing gum, lollipops, whatever she has, her bathing suit slipping off her shoulders as they dig and reach for crackers, juice, pawing the sunglasses from her head. The skipper weaves through the deck indicating life jackets beneath the cushioned bench, Roy's wife breezing by, did we pack enough sandwiches, I can't find Jack's no-mayo. The wife has a nose whittled thin and a voice that lilts low in register before trailing off. Roy says they have everything they could possibly want right here. Clear the aisle, the skipper says. Roy performs the big green salute. Their college mascot was an anthropomorphic beer keg, but she was never up on school spirit, was only filled with Roy's overachieving sperm her senior year.

Fertility was another thing she'd taken for granted. One night, a party or not even, a casual hang in an off-campus house stuffed with trash-salvaged furniture and a pair of milk crates, the season, fall, that one week of prime leaves before interminable winter, couch greased with beer and knee backs and newsprint and sweat. Laura is not sure how she wound up there. She entered parties the way she entered most things in college, with a mix of curiosity and ennui, like sampling a vaguely repulsive pairing of food, whipped cream with oatmeal, or tuna and peanut butter, just to see how the effect would play on the palate. Roy was attractive in a textbook way, iron arms, thick neck, and Laura gravitated toward people like this, whose physicality could either protect her from outside elements or shatter her to pieces. At the party, he flirted with her in a knowing, indiscriminate fashion, casting a wide net the way tuna fishers trapped the idle, unwitting dolphin, no big. There are bound to be accidents. She was there. She was drinking. Her feet stuck to the floor. It was interesting to gauge how much she could pour into herself before her bladder protested, breaking the seal. She was a vessel. Her tolerance was disproportionate to her size. They'd lived in the same dorm freshman year so he wasn't a total stranger.

When he leaned into her, she told herself with the right cowboy boots and the right shorts he could be an early era Bill Murray, yodeling on a bike in the woods. This tapped her curiosity. She wanted to see how he tasted, shove her tongue down the scratchy flesh of his throat and nudge loose the saucy beads of sloppy Joe from his molars, she wanted to pull on his three foot bong and hose that tray of powder cut like suburban fence posts, and she wanted him to hunger for her in return and also not, to see her as a body and absent of body, for what they were: two anchorless souls colliding in the most abjectly human, intimate yet impersonal of ways.

Like that, they fucked, once twice, she threw up in his bathroom, wiped her mouth on a washcloth that smelled of mildew and bleach, squeezed his torqued up toothpaste to shellac her gums with mint. Maybe he walked in on her hunched over the toilet, maybe it was his roommate who found her mid-retch and held back her hair in his fist, sweeping it across his beard like a bouquet of dried sage.

The abortion, like everything else, she approached as novelty. Rode the bus in winter, tires crunching through a foot of fresh snow, frost spreading like a virus across the glass until she could not see out, and thought: this is what makes me! As much as it was an uninspired thought, it was honest: Laura was an acquisitive girl of a certain privilege. There were life experiences to collect. She pinched her wrist to remind herself that this was happening to her and not to someone else. The person in the adjacent seat was a mouth breather and a knitter, her needle dipping in and out of her chaste hand, which made Laura think of that well-traveled joke about marriage and armchair coverlets. She even said: Do you know the one about the crocheted doilies? The woman said, One what, dear? So Laura fell quiet again.

At the clinic, she rustled down along the butcher paper, kept her socks on in the stirrups. They were the red stripe and heather stitch of sock monkey, as if a lovey had been disemboweled then reconfigured onto her feet. The process was cold and crampy but then it was over and Laura had lived through it, was living in the gerund sense. *Behold Laura in the world!* She imagined picking up the phone and calling girls from high school: long distance at Boulder, Maryland, at Emory, but thought better of it, leaving the incident to tunnel inside and callus over, like a spongy layer of moss masking a sinkhole. It was adult. She was capable. Laura heard stories about other girls, girls who waited, paralyzed by guilt or indecision, less fortunate girls, girls without access or immediate funds who saw their bellies stretch into a second trimester. Recently, a big media personality locked seven figures off a memoir that engaged such ethics. But Laura had taken care of herself efficiently—six weeks, barely a heartbeat, nothing more than a mush of cells. Later, she'd stab herself black and blue with needles of progesterone and wish she could have harvested away better parts of herself for when she truly needed them.

Roy sticks out his hand. The catamaran snags a wave and his cap flies off, sailing into the air. He leaps for it, and his belly drops out of his shirt, exposing a happy trail she doesn't remember, but he misses, which is fine because at that moment the engine heaves a sputtering exhale and stills, his hat bopping on the surface beside a lone seagull, easily within reach. She is surprised to see he still has good hair.

"Jessica Pine, right?" Which is amazing, as Evan just called her name, but it doesn't take listening skills to make it at the Ivys. Nor does it take a name to impregnate a classmate and yet somehow he recalls a first and last. Jessica Pine, now she must have been someone. What had she done with her bachelor's degree? The men are trading contacts, making plans for dinner, for playdates, the kids roughly the same age; can you believe?

"Were you econ?" He says without glancing up, punching letters. A pale scar runs along his isthmus between thumb and forefinger. For an instant, Laura longs for that raw fumble of desire before a rote choreography sets in. How messy it can be, how beautiful when you don't know what you're doing. They'd slept diagonally in a tangle of unwashed sheets.

"You have a strawberry on your ass," Laura says. Matter of fact, blunt affect, like a Tourette's tic, but Abortion Roy looks up. "Weird, gross, Mom," she hears. Evan raises a brow as if to say: Honestly? This is the best you can do? The twins—Roy's twins—dodged that one, come around for an adjustment of their straps. His wife tugs on his sleeve. How does *she* know?

The boat rocks in place, the motion unsettling. If there's a flicker of recognition on his part, she misses it, busy as she is pushing down the oceanic swells. In another life, this is the moment she'd puke.

"Joke," she defuses, awkward shrug, and everyone laughs, dismissing her pitiful attempt at humor.

Tonight at the hotel, she'll tag them in a post, arms looped, beach sarongs, staggered by height and hair color, filtered through dramatic cool: Sea la Vie. Long Live the Class of 1993.

Now, flip-flops gather like bones at her feet. Shirts are shed, chests a bright white. Snorkeling gear resembles gas masks. The men pitch over the side with a splash, lift their arms to catch their flapping, commanding children. Roy's wife tosses off her wide-brimmed hat.

"Don't you swim?"

"Live a little," Roy hollers. "Water's great!"

Laura parts her lips.

"She gets cold," Evan says. The wife shrugs. Laura stretches out her legs on the ledge, connecting her constellation of sunspots with a fingernail. Families kick their flippers, plastic tubes poking up for air. She imagines what they see: tropical parrotfish, sea turtles, school of steel-pointed barracuda.

In the distance the island beckons. Laura bridges her eyes. The place looks like paradise, but it's not undiscovered. It holds an exclusive contract with the resort's catamaran company. Porters in floral crowns manufacture cocktails beneath a tiki hut, silver trays gleaming. When they dock, she will walk the plank onto the plush hot sand where drinks and ponies and slow-moving iguanas and french fries in Styrofoam and deep, deadening naps beneath the mangroves await.

THE POLISH GIRL

The Polish Girl hits the jackpot when she clinches the summer job in the South of France. The ad says *Polish Girl*, and she answers. She can be anyone people want her to be. It just so happens she's in Poland visiting a great-aunt on her mother's side who's fallen and shattered her hip. The woman's got to be pushing 100. If she were a horse they'd put her down. Instead, she's high on pillows and morphine.

The Polish Girl is proxy for her mother who can't just abandon her life, whereas the Polish Girl hasn't started hers. A roll with butter, her mother says, in Polish. May everything be as easy as spooning pudding through the thin lips of a distant relative who has nobody else. One meal in and out comes her phone. The girl scrolls. The ad pops. Her mother is Polish, which makes the Polish Girl legit, even if she is an American from Monmouth, New Jersey.

She has the look, which is the employer's top priority. Blonde, blue eyes. Sometimes when she gets restless or bored, the Polish Girl dyes her hair. It takes color like a sponge, soaking up whatever store-bought hue is thrust upon it. Currently, she's all washed out. But she is young and unattached and already overseas. She has everything the employer wants in a domestic. She has a bit of herpes, too, but it's dormant during the video interview.

The French employer does not speak Polish, which is a relief as the Polish Girl speaks only in food terms and idioms. *Don't call a wolf from the forest. Did you fall from a Christmas tree?* English is their common tongue. She can pull off a Polish accent in English by channeling her mother. In Monmouth, her mother cleans houses, sometimes three a day. Word spreads like a match in the Pine Barrens: she is fast, efficient. She never complains.

The caretaking property is located near St. Tropez, which sounds both tropical and acrobatic to the girl, who's never been to France, where she's headed now with a thick cup of tomato juice and complimentary airline socks. In Nice, she gathers stones on the beach and orders an iced coffee that's served hot while she waits for the bus then has to pee the entire ride, so she crosses and uncrosses her legs, the seaside bright and crackling blue.

The house is enormous. Her employer calls it a villa. There are trellises everywhere strangled in vine, heavy with fruit. The Polish Girl has never seen anything like it. Well, she's seen Instagram. In Monmouth, they live in a tract complex by the raceway. She takes classes, sometimes. The vet tech outfits are cute.

"Is it all yours?" she asks her employer, a silver-haired woman in a coral bustier and chiffon bell skirt. There are two hefty cuff bracelets on her wrists, as if she's just busted free.

"Speak only when addressed," her employer says, tapping a cigarette from her soft pack. She blows, waves a hand, as if to say, divorce is a business like any other. "A place like this must come with a girl, don't you see?"

The Polish Girl sees. Grounds ripple in the golden light. The grand tour reveals, for all its Frenchness, an African bazaar inside. There are animal skins on the floors and tusks on the walls and ebony busts trussed in orange headdresses framing the sideboard. Their eyes, inlaid with ivory, stare in reproach, knowing, if given the chance, she would colonize, too. Her great-aunt had been no Warsaw savior. Elephant totems watch over every room.

"For posterity," her employer explains, kissing her on both cheeks before leaving.

The Polish Girl sweeps dead bugs in preparation, mops tile, draws the curtains. She talks aloud to hear herself. One toilet has a tassel flush. All shower nozzles are handheld. The first time she uses one she gets off, hard and quick.

Her employer calls from her Paris flat. "Are you ready?"

The Polish Girl knows from her mother: only missteps attract notice. If the job's done right, she is invisible.

"Yes," she says. Ready or not.

Vacationers arrive. They are German, Spanish, Italian. The Polish Girl greets them at the door with a silver tray of strawberries and champagne. She wears uniform white, her collar open to her crucifix, her only accessory, tasteful not flashy. She has washed the linens, watered the plants, stocked the fridge, leaving out the butter to soften for morning toast. She has never cleaned so hard. Back home her room is a dump. She can't be bothered. Put away crap and there's only more crap. But in the Cote D'Azur (as her employer calls it), she vibrates with fastidious energy. She runs around, running baths, unpacking luggage. She drips essential oil onto every lamp with a pipette.

After her first day, she collapses onto her cot face first. The room's barrenness makes her think of her great-aunt, nicknamed The Squealer for how many neighbors she ratted out in the war. The

Polish Girl calls the nursing home. A miracle! The Squealer says, I'm healing! As if healing were the same as forgiveness. But then, with the girl's shoddy Polish, it's possible some of this is misunderstood.

She makes a natural Polish girl. Maybe it's genetic. Maybe she has finally applied herself. The best part is not thinking. What is there to think about? Her clothes are picked out, her hair braided tight to her scalp in long ropes.

Mostly, she stays out of sight. When they call, she comes. The Americans are the most demanding. They complain about the feel of the towels. They complain when the baguettes go stale. She smiles. She is the Polish Girl who comes with the house, a veritable Janet from that show she binged, so she gathers more bread, more citronella, more brie. Her employer left her a bicycle with a basket for this purpose. Her herpes flares in the sun. It's a painful reminder.

Fathers linger in dark hallways. Their armpits smell like seaweed, their mouths fresh with presumption about Polish girls. She ducks into the children's room, straightens their toys, escorts them to the patio with their Barbies. By accident on purpose she tosses Barbie into the pool. Now they all have to swim. The Polish Girl snags the biggest float. It is a metallic gold donut shimmering with colored sprinkles. The Polish Girl closes her eyes and drifts. For a moment, she is nowhere and everywhere, light dancing on her lids, until the oldest child capsizes her. Little shit, she catches herself. *Kurwa*. The Polish Girl is dripping wet.

If the children want cucumbers, she washes the cucumbers. If the children want grapes, she peels the grapes, slicing them in half if they are American. French families ignore her, more or less. They know their way around the kitchen and their country. Germans want lemonade for their beer. Everyone wants sunscreen massaged into their backs.

All summer it goes like this. They are groups of cousins, college pals. They track sand from beach clubs large as anthills, leave damp suits on the zebra rug. Her favorite week is when the Dutch men come. They cook and clean and keep to themselves. She washes cum stains from knotted briefs each morning, and that's it, the smell suckle-sweet when it's not meant for her.

At night, guests sit on the terrace overlooking the vineyard. The landscaping has been torn up, heather ravaged by an invasion of wild pigs. After midnight, you can hear them rut and snort. The men dare each other to hunt, to slaughter, to roast one on a spit. They get drunk, but only the Americans show it. Italians pour her wine like water. Americans become raunchy and loud, thinking she does not understand. Thinking she is Polish. The fathers talk about hitting that. One father says, But did you see her face? Who knows what you'll catch.

The Polish Girl looks in the mirror. She needs Valtrex and does not know how to order a script, but it's right there on the pharmacy shelf, same name and everything. She pockets a lipstick as she pays and feels, for a second, like she's back in New Jersey.

When guests go out, she turns down their bedding, placing chocolates on the pillows. The Italians leave heaps of dishes in the sink. No matter the hour, they are always eating, which means the Polish Girl is always cleaning. Leaning over the basin, her fingers prune, a water mark stripes her waist. But they make up for their mess with wine. "It is no bother," the Polish Girl says, drinking. Her throat warms. When the Italians leave their hair in the drain, she doesn't mind pulling it out.

The majority are American because the villa is exorbitant and Americans like to believe the more they pay the more special they are. The Polish Girl has to keep up the accent, the halting English. It is tiresome but she is convincing. Maybe she'll become an actor. Maybe she'll be one of those actors that play patients in medical school. She could fake a stroke. While they're out stocking up on truffle honey and herbes de Provence, she finds a tin of marijuana mints on a bedside table, so now she is sky high and twirling, the hills are alive in the late day sun. Never in a million years would she have pictured herself here, so the Polish Girl snaps a selfie just to prove it, before sobering up on a pasty log of chèvre.

That evening, a female guest joins her in the kitchen, chatting and drying dishes, and it's so nice, the Polish Girl nearly blows her cover.

"I didn't grow up with help," the woman says, which snaps the Polish Girl back into her role.

"You must to take easy." She refills the woman's glass. "Enjoy in yourself, Missus. Go. Go make the laughter and the light."

"It is impossible."

"Everything is possible."

The woman looks at her with terrific pity before wandering out.

Men walk in on her in the bathroom. Men walk into her sleeping quarters. Doh, they say. Thought this was the pool house. They leave the nubs of their Cubans outside her room, like dogs marking their territory. They stare too long at her tits. They are used to getting what they want. One man grabs her wrist. "I'm onto you," he says. The Polish Girl bites her lip so hard her viral scab bleeds.

The sky fills with tiny stars. She empties ashtrays and listens. They are talking about fucking without kissing. Her face gets hot. They haven't kissed their wives in years.

They say this, like it's a badge of honor. They call it the beauty of marriage.

When they go on day trips to nearby villages, the Polish Girl bikes to the beach. The surf pierces her with a familiar ache. Sunbathers are old and naked, asses flattened from the cruelty of time. Men with their penises out, shrunken stubs dangling between legs. Maybe it's a gay beach. Maybe they are simply inured to her, with her peroxide and sunburn and string bikini. They don't glance her way, not even when she sheds her top. A grandmother tosses a red ball with her grandson, bare breasts bobbing, and she tries to picture her own mother playing catch with her future children, chasing them over the tall, soft dunes.

Friends DM but she's not checking social. Every night is an enviable sunset. She is living the Photoshop. Her mother asks when she is coming home. What? She shouts. Guests are having a dance party. Has an elephant stomped on your ear? Her mother wants to know, in Polish.

By fall, the pace has slowed, and the Polish Girl relishes the quiet. She dries stalks of lavender upside down by a string, runs through the vineyard like a corn maze, plucks grapes more sour than sweet. That is always her problem. Colors turn to hay. Sometimes she takes the bus into town to watch the yachts docked in the off-season. Street artists still set up easels along the pier but the ice cream shops are closed. Tourists wear burkas. They are not sitting for their portraits. This is when she loves Saint-Tropez the most.

Christmas comes and goes. Her great-aunt dies in her sleep. Sepsis, the nursing home says. Her blood had turned toxic with infection from the break. The Polish Girl surprises herself by crying. No love lost for The Squealer, but still. Any sort of end contains its own grief.

On New Year's Day, she watches the ball drop from her phone, remembers wearing diapers in the drunken mob with the other bridge-and-tunnelers. What they don't tell you until after you've been corralled and locked in place is you can't hear the performances from blocks away. There's no JumboTron or anything. Post Malone looks like a guy she once knew. Times Square is not a party but a waiting around, having to pee. In the south of France she is hours ahead. Already the Polish Girl knows better.

Like so much of her life, it happens slowly then all at once. Winter settles into the region. It is cold, but she teaches herself how to build a fire, tossing in a copy of *The Sheltering Sky* left behind by a guest, for the hell of it, which is to say, she isn't really paying attention until she is. Things change. Borders close. She cannot travel, cannot leave. She cannot even ride her bicycle for bread. To the beach. Everyone who can clear out of the south of France clears out. Her employer stops calling. Maybe she is sick. Maybe worse.

The Polish Girl is all alone. With no one to mock her face, no one to push her against a stone wall, to slide a fist beneath her skirted pleats. No employer to ensure she wear white on white. Just her, in the big empty house, with the busts and the pigs and bushels of lavender, her fire burning, the most glorious sunsets she's ever seen.

ABOUT THE AUTHOR

Sara Lippmann is the author of the story collection *Doll Palace*. She was awarded an artist's fellowship in fiction from New York Foundation for the Arts, and her work has appeared in *The Millions, The Washington Post, Best Small Fictions 2020* and elsewhere. She teaches with Jericho Writers and at St. Joseph's College in Brooklyn. Her debut novel, *LECH*, will be published by Tortoise Books later this year. For more, visit www.saralippmann.com.

ACKNOWLEDGMENTS

Thank you to the editors and journals who first saw something in these stories: *Fiction Southeast, Split Lip Magazine, Third Point Press, Epiphany Magazine, storySouth, People Holding, Potomac Review, Midnight Breakfast, New Flash Fiction Review, Heavy Feather Review, Gone Lawn, Atticus Review, Burrow Press, Berfrois, Litro Magazine, Synaesthesia Magazine, Vol.1 Brooklyn,* and *Squalorly.* Thank you, internet. Thank you, readers. To my agent, Jenni Ferrari-Adler, and to the entire team at Mason Jar Press—Ian Anderson, Ashley Miller, Heather Rounds, and Michael Tager—who have brought so much joy, professionalism, wisdom, and vision to this project. To Steve Almond, Danielle Lazarin, Bud Smith, Marcy Dermansky, Taylor Byas, Robert Lopez, and Karen Pittelman for taking the time from their very full lives to look at these pages, and whose generosity is a raft. To Penina Roth, for her energy and support, and to every writer who's ever trusted me with their work: I love nothing more than to read your words. To beloved jerks: Melanie Pappadis Faranello, Bob Hill, Seth Rogoff, Karen & the Sorrows, Yvonne Conza, Meg Tuite, Nita Noveno, Brian Gresko, Julie Innis, Shasta Grant, Rachel Sherman, Josh Rolnick, Ben Tanzer, Erika Dreifus, Zeeva Bukai, The Rumble Ponies, Shayne Terry,

Alice Kaltman, Maureen Langloss, and Christopher Gonzalez, for making it a little less lonely in the hole, to Dana, Ann, and all the girls of then and now, and to Tamara, Micki, Rachel, Holly, Esther, Elissa, for the walks, talks, and runs. To my sister, Elisa, for being there, always, and to my family, for loving me even though I never made it to medical school, to the Feigs and Rosenthals: for taking me in as one of your own; to my children who light up my life, my dog who holds no judgment, and to Rob who holds my heart.

OTHER TITLES FROM MASON JAR PRESS

The Monotonous Chaos of Existence
short stories by Hisham Bustani

Peculiar Heritage
poetry DeMisty D. Bellinger

Call a Body Home
short stories chapbook by Michael Alessi

The Horror is Us
an anthology of horror fiction edited by Justin Sanders

Suppose Muscle Suppose Night Suppose This in August
memoir by Danielle Zaccagnino

Ashley Sugarnotch & the Wolf
poetry by Elizabeth Deanna Morris Lakes

...and Other Disasters
short stories by Malka Older

All Friends Are Necessary
a novella by Tomas Moniz

Learn more at masonjarpress.com